To Sharel,

*Always let your
heart be Captured
by God!*

Captured

[signature]

By Terri J. Haynes

BROWN GIRLS BOOKS

Houston, Texas * Washington, D.C. * Raleigh/Durham, NC

Captured © 2015 by Terri J. Haynes

Brown Girls Faith

Brown Girls Publishing,

LLC www.browngirlspublishing.com

ISBN Ebook: 9781625174291

ISBN Print: 9781625179678

First Brown Girls Publishing LLC trade printing

Manufactured and Printed in the United States of America

Advance Praise for Captured

"Terri Haynes rips news from today's most fascinating headlines to craft a novel filled with heart-tugging twists and turns. Readers won't want this book to end. Devour each page to be intrigued and enthralled."
~ Stacy Hawkins Adams,
author of *The Someday List* and *Finding Home.*

"In her latest novel, Terri Haynes takes readers inside the horrific world of human trafficking. If you're looking for a suspenseful page-turner mixed with action and a sweet budding romance, Haynes' *Captured* should be on your to-read list."
~ Tyora Moody, author of the *Serena Manchester Series* and *Victory Gospel Series*

Dedication

To Sharon Sanchez:
I am blessed to have known you. I am heartbroken that
you're gone.

Acknowledgements

Life in Christ is the greatest story ever. It's even better when you have other characters to enjoy the tale with you. To my cast of characters:

Abrian E. Haynes, the Wonderhubby. I know when you married me you didn't realize the adventure you were getting into. I loved the first 20 years of being your wife. Let's do 20 more. Thanks for being my pastor, support system, cheerleader, handler, culinary support, knitting partner and Bajan Bully. I love you.

Jazmyne, Dartanyon and Emmanuel, I love you all so dearly. I'm so thankful and honored that God chose me to be your mom. It means so much to know that you're proud of me because I am so proud of you guys. Bust a cap, the dogs came bounding over and Hail Hydra.

To Linda Sothern. You are the best editor a girl could ask for. You're not just a champion for my writing, but for me. Although I fuss about your corrections, I know you want me to be the best writer I can be. I'm looking forward to sharing the rest of my stories and all my extra conjunctions with you.

To Kim Ross, my sister-friend, always the straight shooter. I love your honesty and love having a fellow artist to share my passion with. Thank you for the encouragement and threats. To Jake and Kristy Greene, thanks for the prayers. I appreciate them and you.

Daddy, I'm still in awe that you kept my stories in your wallet when I was a kid. Thank you for validating my gift. Wanda, Lisa, Michelle, and Sherrie, we've produced a generation of super-readers. Keep up the good work.

Thank you to my editor, Rhonda McKnight. A little polish and you made my manuscript shine. Thanks for believing in my manuscript. I'm looking forward to the rest of our journey together.

I thank God, whose timing is always perfect, especially when we don't understand it. He gave me a gift, storytelling, and allowed me to use it for His glory.

Chapter 1

One thousand and ninety five days of soul draining disregard for human life. *Sixty-four more days shouldn't be that hard.* Then the real challenge would begin.

Special Agent Will Anderson took his position behind a parked car, giving him a full view of the brothel the FBI and SWAT team were prepared to raid. Two of his fellow agents from the Civil Rights Division of the FBI joined the SWAT officers huddled on the porch. In the silence of the NW DC neighborhood, they took steps so quiet that Will couldn't hear them even though they stood about one hundred feet away. The point man gestured placement instructions and the group shifted, still not making a sound.

Breathing in the cool, moist April air, Will braced himself on the hood of the car and raised his weapon. He cataloged everything he saw in front of him, particularly doors and windows. He and another SWAT team member were tasked to ensure no one in the house escaped.

Once the entry team went in, people tended to fly in every direction. He'd seen grown men dive off roofs to avoid capture. If someone did, Will would be waiting.

As essential as his job was, Will fought the feeling of being left behind. When he had been assigned to this team, a surprising sense of purpose replaced the constant uselessness he felt. His pending transfer cloaked him in an invisibility shield and Will spent most of his days idle…unless there was busywork no one else wanted. Unfortunately, all those good feelings evaporated when he learned he'd be on lookout.

The point-man held up his hand and gave the team a 3-2-1 countdown. Will's muscles tensed as the countdown hit one and the team used a ram to bust down the door. An agent stepped forward and tossed two flash bombs into the gaping hole where the door once stood. Things were about to get lively. The team rushed in, their shouts mingling with the shouts of those inside. A second loud bang went off as the other half of the team entered the back of the house, effectively trapping all the occupants inside. Unless one of them wanted to risk the windows.

No sooner than the second bang stopped ringing in Will's ears, the sound of breaking glass replaced it. His head snapped up in time to see a man running across the grass toward the driveway.

Adrenaline surged and Will sprang from his hiding spot. "FBI!" He leveled his weapon at the man.

The man skidded to a stop. Will approached him with quick scissor steps. "Turn around."

The man shifted, arms slightly extended from his body. Latino male, approximately 30-35 years old. He stood level to Will's 6'1" height, his loose clothing and the evening's dim lighting making it hard to accurately judge his weight. He was possibly twenty pounds heavier than Will. That could be crucial if this arrest turned physical, but since the man was unarmed, it probably wouldn't come to that.

Will took one more step toward the man. "Let me see your hands."

The man obeyed, stretching out his arms far enough for his sleeves to rise. Tattoos covered his entire right forearm. Will stared at the detailed artwork, fought a feeling of familiarity, and returned his attention to the man.

Interestingly, the man's expression had brightened. He almost seemed ready to smile. He tilted his head to the side. "Nice to see you again, Officer Anderson."

Will gripped his weapon tighter. *How did. . .* "Turn around."

The man chuckled. "I guess I should call you Agent Anderson. Looks like you've moved on to better things since you left Baltimore."

Beads of sweat formed on the back of Will's neck as he studied the man. *Who is this guy?* He didn't stand out from all the suspects Will had arrested over the years. The guy had given him a clue though. They'd crossed paths in Baltimore, which required Will to dig even deeper into his memory.

"Don't remember me?" The man's smirk grew. "I'm disappointed. I remember you. You nearly ruined me." The man laughed. "I'm going to enjoy returning the favor."

Will reached into one of the pockets of his vest and pulled out a zip cuff. "I said turn around."

The man shrugged and began to turn.

"Put your hands behind your back." Will moved to cuff him, but before he could, the man whipped around. In one fluid movement, the man lunged forward and grabbed Will's wrist. He twisted it hard. Pain jarred up Will's arm and down his fingertips. Dropping the zip cuff, Will threw a roundhouse punch with his free hand. The blow connected with the man's chin. The impact cracked Will's knuckles and forced the man backward.

The man swayed, regained his balance and brought his booted foot up in a front kick that landed between the W and A in the center of Will's SWAT vest. Air rushed out of Will's lungs and he doubled over. The light from the house swirled in little circles on the grass. The man pivoted and took off running down the side of the house.

Will forced himself upright, struggling to grip his weapon. His chest refused to expand to let in another breath, no matter how hard he fought. *I can't let this guy get away.* He lifted his left arm and braced his aching hand on it. The man had reached the back of the house and would disappear into the woods in two seconds. Will took a deep breath, steadied himself, and fired two shots.

He didn't see the man go down as much as he heard him. Breath slowly returning to his lungs, Will pushed forward. The man scrambled up from the ground and shuffled to the tree line of the backyard with a limp. Will trotted behind him, vision spinning, but the man disappeared beyond his view. Will let out a loud grunt and two agents emerged from the back of the house.

"You all right?"

Will dragged in a breath and nodded. "A suspect got away. I hit him."

"Which way did he go?" One of the agents charged down the steps and paused just long enough for Will to point in the direction the suspect went. The other agent followed.

If Will's shot was good, which the darkness made it impossible to ascertain, the agent should find the man nearby and bleeding. Either way, Will would have to figure out how a suspect in a brothel raid knew his name.

*

Savannah Elliott arrived at the front door to her human rights organization, *Plateau*, at 10:30am exactly. She took a deep breath and short pause before opening the door and launching into her day. She'd started almost every day like this, ready to attack her to-do list the minute she stepped in the door.

When people asked her how she'd managed to build a successful non-profit in just a year, she gave the answer she'd lived: hard work and dedication.

Her powerwalk slowed as she passed the front desk. It sat unmanned. She checked the clock on the wall. Ten-thirty. Where in the world was her receptionist, Carrie? A hint of worry shuddered through her. *Stop it. She's probably in the break room getting coffee.* She headed toward her office and noticed all the other offices were empty. Worry notched up, tightening her stomach.

She detoured and continued down the hall listening for any sounds that might give her a clue as to where they'd all gone. She rounded a corner past the break room and spotted Carrie, along with her other employees, Jim, Chelsea, and Abby, crowded around the television in the conference room. She exhaled.

Carrie looked up when Savannah entered the room. She gestured toward the television. "Have you seen this?"

Savannah eased between Carrie and Jim. The screen flashed from the newscaster to a shot of a wooded area. FBI agents surveyed a site with several white sheets erected around it. Savannah studied the trees, a twinge of familiarity hedging her mind.

"Investigators have only begun the long process of identifying the remains found yesterday," reported the voiceover. "Authorities say it may take months or years, if ever."

"Where is this?" Savannah asked.

Carrie eyed her. "You don't recognize your home state?"

Savannah set her purse on the conference table. "A mass grave in Georgia?"

"Yes, Ware County," Jim said. "Good place to hide some bodies. Pretty rugged out there."

Mass graves normally meant one of two things: organized crime or human trafficking. Improbable that the grave pointed to organized crime. Not a big problem in Georgia. It had to be human trafficking. That thought caused her breath to catch. Mass graves also meant something else: victims no one helped.

Once the news story ended and her staff dispersed, Savannah flipped the channel to CNN. They didn't offer much more info than the local stations but any details were valuable. The graves were found a few days ago, which meant that the FBI had only begun to process the evidence. The bodies were discovered in a container of some kind, buried deep in state-owned land. The newscast didn't mention what kind of container or what condition the bodies were in.

Savannah flipped off the TV and went to her office. Things were about to get interesting for the governor of Georgia…and by default, her. How could a mass grave not affect Governor James Elliott, especially since his daughter ran a non-profit to combat human trafficking? As much as he and her mother might not approve of her life choices, he would call and ask for her help to save face.

She took her place at her desk and waited for the phone to ring. A stack of new phone messages sat on top of some files. One was from the liaison of the DC Human Trafficking Taskforce.

The message, in Carrie's smooth handwriting, stated that a brothel was raided the night before. They needed Savannah to consult with a victim, Marisol Benitez, who was currently in a hospital in NW. She rose from her desk. Guess her father would have to leave a message.

Chapter 2

Will carefully balanced his cup of coffee in his sore hand as he sank into his chair. Both he and the chair let out a groan. The ibuprofen he'd taken earlier hadn't done much to dull the pain in his chest. After an exam and an x-ray, the doctor in the ER had cleared him to go home and rest for a few days. He could have gone home for a week and it wouldn't matter. No one had noticed that he hadn't gotten into the office until almost 3pm.

He set the coffee cup on his nearly empty desk next to a manila folder with a bright orange Post-it note. He glanced at his desk's sparse décor, his gaze falling on a picture of a brown-eyed boy. He studied the child's gapped smile. Jordan hadn't been happy about taking his second grade portrait with missing teeth. But it perfectly embodied everything that made Jordan special, right down to his crooked half grin. Will lifted the frame. He'd give anything to hold Jordan in his arms. He shoved the desire into his mind's recesses. To survive the next two months, it would have to remain there. He deposited the photo into a box, careful not to let it plunk to the bottom.

Now his desk couldn't be emptier.

Will took a deep breath and eyed the folder. The Post-it note read, *Do your thing.* He recognized the square handwriting of his boss, Special Agent Dan Carter. He also recognized that his boss had assigned him an interview. *Doing his thing* was getting the most frightened, distrustful victims to give a statement. Will smirked at his reputation. Sadly, other agents didn't realize he didn't have a *thing* beyond genuine compassion. No superpower there.

He opened the folder. The first page was the note on the house raid the night before. Twenty-five girls, with no identification, living in squalor and being used for prostitution. More notable, all of them appeared to be foreigners. Most of the trafficking cases Will had seen in his years in DC tended to be US citizens trafficked from another state. The number of girls, twenty-five was unusually high, added to the uniqueness of the raid. Will sighed. Most of them were too ill to talk, except one: Marisol Benitez. She was at Washington Hospital Center in NW, DC being treated for a myriad of problems.

Marisol. He planted her name in his mind.

Marisol, someone's daughter.

He rose slowly, put on his jacket, and headed to the parking garage. Washington Hospital Center was only fifteen-minutes away, but the drive took almost thirty. Metro rush hour didn't play by the rules on days like today.

Sixth Street was already clogged with cars, probably from the perpetual construction on New York Avenue. Will watched the other cars buck like broncos, trying to speed in the short spaces.

He drummed his fingers on the steering wheel. *Can this go any faster?* He moved forward a half of car length. *Apparently not.*

Trapped…there was nothing he could do about it. Even if he allowed his frustration to balloon into anger, he would still be hedged in on every side. Jordan's portrait popped into his mind. Anger didn't change anything. He had thrown several angry fits about Jordan and nothing changed. Now he was inching forward to his transfer, one slow day at a time.

Will finally whipped his car into the hospital's parking garage, climbed out, and took the elevator up to the ground floor. Several meanderers crowded the hallway in front of him. He snorted. More traffic.

He maneuvered around them and then switched to his power-walk. Sunlight streamed through the lobby's floor-to-ceiling front windows. Will flashed his badge at the visitor's desk and asked for Marisol Benitez's room. The receptionist directed him to the third floor and he took the elevator up. The disinfectant smell, stronger than in the lobby, wafted to his nose and he suppressed a shudder. He nodded as he passed nurses in the hall. Marisol's door stood slightly ajar. He knocked twice.

A stocky MPD officer greeted him. "Special Agent Anderson." The man's meaty handshake enveloped Will's fingers. "I'm Officer Grant."

Will followed him to the foot of the bed where Marisol lay. Monitor cords snaked down to her frail body. Mottled patches of skin covered most of her honey tone.

Each breath slightly rattled when she exhaled. Her black hair spread across the pillow in a tangled mess that would make Medusa envious. She gave Will a quick, glassy-eyed assessment. The trade industry had sucked the beauty out of her. She had the face of someone who'd lived fifty years of heartache in only eighteen.

Will steadied himself for the delicate balancing act of interviewing victims. It needed both compassion and assertiveness. Marisol's ragged breaths threatened to tip the scales all the way to compassion. She needed rest and counseling, but he needed to catch the bad guy.

Balance.

Will adjusted his jacket and noticed the woman at Marisol's bedside. Her long brown hair, with subtle highlights, curled in soft ringlets that fell into her face. Her yellow suit perfectly complemented her creamy café latte skin and accentuated her shape without revealing too much.

She flashed Will a slight smile.

His mouth went dry and he ground his teeth together to keep his jaw from dropping.

He recovered as Officer Grant did the introductions. "Special Agent Anderson, this is Savannah Elliott, a member of the DC Task Force. Her center helps victims of human trafficking."

Ms. Elliott looked Will straight in the eye and gave him a firm handshake. "Nice to meet you, Agent Anderson." *Soft hands and confident.* Her melodious Southern accent surprised him. A pleasant surprise.

Will nodded, not sure his voice wouldn't squeak like a teenage boy, but inserted a mental wall of professionalism between he and Savannah…no, Ms. Elliott.

Ms. Elliott spoke to Marisol in Spanish. In the middle of the sentence, she said Will's name. Marisol twitched, the only acknowledgement she'd heard.

"Hello, Marisol." Will measured out his tone to ribbon smoothness.

Someone's daughter.

Marisol didn't respond.

"Do you want to take the lead?" Officer Grant asked.

"You go ahead." Always best to yield to professional courtesy. Besides, some other agent would probably take over the investigation and see it to the end.

Will slid into the room's remaining chair and Officer Grant began the questions. He asked about the men who'd run the brothel, how long she'd been in the United States and for her identification. Officer Grant lobbed inquiry after inquiry at Marisol, his impatient tone grating at Will's nerves.

Within five minutes, Will's frustration with traffic paled in comparison to Officer Grant's assault questioning. Marisol hadn't run a red light or jaywalked. She was a victim. She'd lived through horrors that would send Officer Grant home crying to his mother.

Marisol only stared at the small tent her toes made at the end of the bed.

Officer Grant folded his arms. "This is going nowhere. Tell her that she'll be deported if she doesn't cooperate."

"When working with traffic victims, it takes time to gain their trust. It's not wise to threaten them." Ms. Elliott spoke without the slightest hint of emotion but her eyes narrowed. A gesture so slight that if Will had blinked, he would have missed it.

Officer Grant got her message loud and clear. He slightly dropped his head.

Nicely done, Ms. Elliott.

Will stood but didn't move any closer to the bed. "Do you mind if I ask a few questions?"

Officer Grant let out a huff. "Go ahead if you think you can do better."

I'm sure I can do better. "Marisol, I know you may be frightened, I need your help." Will kept his voice low and softened his tone. He didn't have to go extra soft since Officer Grant had set the stage for him to be the good cop. "I need to catch those men to make sure they don't hurt anyone else."

Marisol's eyes shifted to him for a second.

Will took out his pen and notepad and stepped closer to the bed, putting himself between Marisol and Officer Grant. "What is the last date you remember before you were brought here?"

Silence. Officer Grant shifted behind him but Will remained still, pen poised over his notepad. Marisol didn't respond after Ms. Elliott translated. Seconds of silence ticked by. Will's hope slipped. *Come on, Marisol. You can do it.* He waited a minute more. Just as he considered trying another approach, Marisol spoke. With the little Spanish he knew, he managed to catch one word. *Diciembre.* She'd been in the country for four months. A relatively short time for traffic victims, but long enough for her to live through years worth of horror.

Ms. Elliott turned to him. "December 3rd."

Will looked at Marisol. "Thank you. Where are you from?"

To his surprise, tears formed in the girl's eyes as she responded.

Ms. Elliott reached over and pulled a tissue from the box at the bedside and handed it to her. "She says she's from Guatemala."

Will made note of that on his pad. "Do you know the men who brought you here?"

He watched Marisol's slightly open expression close again as Ms. Elliott spoke. *Wrong question, Anderson.* But there was information even in that closed expression. With her reaction, Will wondered if she did in fact know the people who lured her into coming to the States illegally. Making promises of a grand life in America was one of the more popular tactics that traffickers used. They often met with the girls several times before they actually arranged transport.

"Marisol, don't worry. You're safe now."

When Ms. Elliot translated, Marisol burst into tears. Will exerted superhuman effort not to give her a comforting touch, but he knew it would be better if he didn't. Ms. Elliott, on the other hand, wasted no time grasping the girl's hands and speaking softly to her. Marisol's response came through choked sobs.

Ms. Elliott glanced over her shoulder at Will. "She said that the men told her that she should never talk to the police because they will put her in jail."

Another common tactic and Officer Grant probably didn't help Marisol's opinion of law enforcement. "Let her know I won't put her in jail."

Savannah relayed the message but Marisol's tears increased. Soon she was coughing uncontrollably. Will stepped back. The stress of this interview wasn't helping. "I think this is enough for now. She could probably use the rest."

Ms. Elliott nodded. "We don't want to overwhelm her."

Officer Grant shook his head. "Rest from what? She certainly didn't overexert herself."

Will fisted his hands, trying to squeeze the fire out of his anger.

Ms. Elliott turned and spoke in soft tones to Marisol. The girl nodded at certain points, the tenseness in her arms melting away. Will listened for a moment more. Ms. Elliott was good. He took a deep breath, some of his own stress abating.

Will exited the room and Officer Grant followed him into the hallway.

"Unbelievable." Officer Grant rubbed his hand over his face.

Will shoved his hands in his pockets, the safest place for them. He stepped closer so he and Officer Grant stood eye-to-eye. "I don't think your interrogation helped."

"She's in the country illegally. She was found in a house with other illegals and she won't give us any information. What am I supposed to do, hold her hand?"

Will clinched his jaw. "That might have been more effective. Did you notice that she's ill and obviously abused?"

Officer Grant's eyebrows shot up. "Are you sure you're on the right side of the law? Our job is to catch the bad guys, not babysit."

Will pointed to the door. "Have you ever worked with traffic victims? Without her help, we can't catch bad guys. You would do well to remember that."

"I'll remember that until we figure out how she got in the country, she's breaking the law."

A sharp comeback was already on Will's tongue, but Ms. Elliott's arrival sliced through the argument. Good thing, too.

She stood beside Will wearing a pinched expression. Officer Grant glanced down the hall, mumbled something about needing to leave, and he was gone.

She turned to face Will. "I'm sorry that wasn't more productive."

Up close, Will noticed that her brown eyes swirled like iced tea with lemon. "Me, too."

"Being questioned by Officer Grant didn't help." Ms. Elliott folded her arms across her chest and her nose flared. "Force may work well on your side of the equation, but not on the victim side."

Will offered her a slight smile. "I'm not your enemy, Ms. Elliott."

She paused and nervously tucked her hair behind her ear, sending her diamond and gold hoop earring swaying. Her expression softened. "I know. I'm sorry."

The PA system squawked overhead, drowning out everything except for the blood pounding through Will's ears. Did she know how adorable she was? "Apology accepted."

Ms. Elliott shifted, her eyes sparkling under the hall lights. "I assume you'll want to question her again."

Will inhaled to slow his heart rate. "Yes, preferably without Officer Grant."

She smiled. "Good." She reached in her purse and pulled out a business card. "If you would like, I can translate for you."

I would like. "Great."

They both turned and headed toward the same elevator bank. They waited in silence, but Will couldn't resist stealing glances at her.

He watched her fluid movements as she checked her phone. He'd met all kinds of people dedicated to combating human trafficking, but Ms. Elliott was the oddest of them all. Her mannerisms, gentleness, poise and quite frankly, beauty, seemed incompatible with this kind of work, but at the same time, it fit perfectly. Refreshing compared to all the ugliness.

Once inside the elevator, he pressed the button for the ground floor and Ms. Elliott smiled. "Guess we're going in the same direction."

"Guess so."

They continued their trip together all the way outside. The dark sky hung heavy with remaining clouds from the day. Too dark for a woman to be walking alone. "Ms. Elliott, do you mind if I walk you to your car, since we seem to be parked near each other?"

"I would feel so much better if you did." She smiled, tucked her hair behind her ear again, and batted her eyes at him. "Please call me Savannah."

Will's stomach did a little flip but he suppressed it. *Don't even think about catching feelings.* If he wasn't transferring, he would be all for catching feelings for her.

*

Savannah hitched her purse up to her shoulder and fell in step beside Agent Anderson. The evening air cooled her cheeks. *Really, Savannah? Was that your attempt to flirt?* He was handsome. Maybe law enforcement required that their male recruits be attractive.

She'd seen her share of handsome police officers, ATF, FBI, and ICE agents. Special Agent Anderson stood out from the rest. She'd never seen someone whose eyes, warm brown, matched his skin tone. A sense of calm radiated from him, even though he could be seen as imposing with his height and broad shoulders.

She also liked the fact that he seemed completely at ease with the comfortable silence between them. He didn't feel the need to fill up the moments with idle chatter. Unfortunately, his silence left her with her own thoughts. She'd checked her phone before they entered the elevator. No call from Daddy. Had she misjudged him? A lot had changed in the year she'd been in DC.

Agent Anderson slowed a step behind her, drawing her out of her thoughts. He wore a look of concentration. More concentration than needed for walking through a parking garage, unless he forgot where he'd parked his car.

"Is everything all right?"

He quickly glanced at her and tipped his head to his left in the slightest motion. "Not sure. That car is following us."

Savannah glanced around him. A black Crown Victoria with dark tinted windows eased down the row parallel to them. She hadn't noticed it when they entered the garage. "Are you sure?"

"I'm not. They could be following us for a parking space."

"Maybe."

"But they turned their lights off." He stepped around her, putting himself on the outside of them.

Savannah's heart rate ticked up. The car's erratic behavior could be harmless, but from what she'd seen of Agent Anderson upstairs, she trusted he'd seen something that warranted alarm.

"Where is your car?" he asked as he increased his pace.

The trunk of her little sedan peeked out between two cars ahead of them. "The silver—"

A loud screech echoed through the garage as the Crown Victoria sped up, turned up the row, and zoomed toward them. Even though the car was speeding, time slowed. The passenger side window rolled down and something eased out. It wasn't until Agent Anderson shoved her that she realized it was the barrel of a gun.

She and Agent Anderson tumbled sideways. They slammed into the ground as the first shot boomed, its echo reverberating above their heads.

The second shot sounded. Agent Anderson shielded her with his body. Fear squeezed her heart. Blood pounded in her ears along with Agent Anderson's breathing. She wanted to scream but couldn't find the breath to do it.

Agent Anderson rolled over, and in a flash -- quicker than her eyes could process-- drew his weapon. He popped to his feet and fired three shots at the car.

Savannah scooted against the car nearest her and covered her head with her hands. Tears formed in her eyes.

Everything grew quiet and Agent Anderson's face came into view. "Savannah, are you all right?"

She lowered her hands and managed to nod. Disbelief and fear still closed her throat.

Agent Anderson offered his hand. "Can you stand?"

As he did, she noticed a rip on the sleeve of his suit jacket. Red colored the edges of the tear. She gasped. "You're bleeding."

His attention snapped to his sleeve, disbelief washing over his face. "I am."

Footsteps echoed through the parking garage. Confusion rang in her mind as loud as the approaching sirens. Someone had just tried to kill her...or Agent Anderson. Her head throbbed. Agent Anderson's job definitely put him in the running, but her secrets weighed just as heavily.

Chapter 3

Two doctor's evaluations in two days.

Will sat on the edge of a gurney from the ambulance that arrived shortly after the shooting. He tried not to laugh at the irony of getting injured in a hospital parking lot, but still needing an ambulance. A few doctors had come out to examine him, but by the time they'd gotten to him, the ambulance had arrived.

Savannah stood a few feet from him, arms wrapped around her body, near the car that had shielded them from the shots. A long black smudge marred her yellow skirt. A female MPD officer stood with her, probably asking her questions. Hopefully, MPD would show as much zeal in finding the shooter as Officer Grant exhibited on Marisol. Every so often, Savannah glanced in his direction, her brow furrowed in worry.

He'd worn the same expression before he realized that he'd been hit. When the shots started, instincts kicked in. He'd shoved Savannah to the ground hard, but there she stood, shaken yet unharmed. *She's tougher than she looks.* She would have to be. Someone had just tried to kill one of them. For her sake, Will prayed he was the target.

The officer left Savannah and approached Will as the EMT finished bandaging up his arm.

"How are you, Agent Anderson?" the officer, her nametag read Dunn, asked. Her casual stance and slow movements instantly grated against Will's nerves.

Guess Officer Grant is the only one with any passion in MPD. "Just grazed me. I'll be fine."

"Can you give me a statement?"

Will told her about the car and its odd behavior. He then watched her slowly scrawl the information on her pad. Did she realize that most investigations that were not solved quickly went cold quickly?

"Did you get a make and model."

"Crown Vic. Maybe '98, '99."

Officer Dunn recorded his answer. "Anything else?"

Will focused his memory. "Two black males inside. Mid-twenties and the front right tire was flat."

Officer Dunn snorted. "Okay. Do you know of anyone who would try to hurt you?"

His friend from last night popped into his mind. "I was working a case last night and one of the suspects threatened me." It was a long shot mentioning it. Not likely his guy had time to stage this so soon after being shot, but criminals could be resourceful. A passing mention was enough since Savannah might have been the target, not him.

"I assume that's being handled by the FBI." She closed her notepad. "But if you could keep me in the loop..."

"Of course."

Officer Dunn nodded and sashayed away. Will hopped off the gurney. The minute he did, Savannah rushed to him. He fought a smile.

She reached out and touched him on the forearm below his injury. "How bad is it?"

"Barely a scratch."

Her hand fell away. "I can't believe this."

"Do you have someone to take you home?"

She hugged herself again. "My brother and sister-in-law are coming."

"I'll wait with you until they get here."

Savannah shook her head. "You've already done so much for me. The officers are here and you're injured."

He shrugged. "I don't mind."

She glanced up at him, shadows falling across her face. "Thank you...for saving me."

Will squirmed. Whenever he did something helpful for someone, they wanted to shower him with thanks. He understood their reaction, but hadn't learned to shake the discomfort in accepting gratitude for doing what came naturally. Saving her was more training and instinct than anything else. No, he didn't want to see Savannah hurt, but he also didn't make a conscious thought about pushing her out of the range of the bullets.

He glanced down at his shoes. "You're welcome."

Savannah didn't speak the rest of the time they waited for her brother, which turned out to be thirty minutes longer.

Will watched as her brother, who Savannah strongly favored, sprang from his car as soon as it stopped. Savannah rushed to him and they embraced. A woman Will guessed was Savannah's sister-in-law joined the hug. They appeared to be a loving family.

Speaking of family, his mother, Denise Anderson, would probably react the same way. Even though he would see her tomorrow for their customary weekly dinner, no way he could delay telling her until then. If she found out about the shooting before he told her, she would make her displeasure known. It was a strong possibility she could learn about it on her own since she was the biggest news junkie. There was no way the local news stations wouldn't cover a shooting in a hospital parking lot.

Savannah glanced back at him and waved. He waved back and turned toward his car. He pushed away the false sense of security he felt for Savannah. Yes, she was with her brother, but her nor Will were safe until they figured out why someone had tried to gun them down. Will doubted she was the target. What enemies could she have?

As he walked past the spot where they'd fallen, something glinted from beneath the car. He paused. Did the police miss a shell casing?

He looked over his shoulder for Officer Dunn but didn't see her. He stooped, bracing his arm against his chest, and studied the object. A hoop earring studded with diamonds, one he'd noticed Savannah wearing earlier, sparkled in the faint light of the garage. Had he pushed her that hard?

He picked it up and put it in his pocket. When he climbed into his car, he retrieved the card she'd given him and dialed the number on it. A voicemail message began after one ring and informed him he'd reached Plateau. After the beep, he left a message for Savannah to call him and gave his contact information. Good that she had it just in case someone else decided to shoot at her.

*

Savannah entered the front door of Plateau a little before lunch. She focused on each step but it wasn't enough to hide the slight limp she'd developed overnight. She hadn't felt a thing while she was still at the hospital. Most likely the adrenaline. Once it had worn off, she noticed all sorts of aches and pains.

Her brother, Joshua, had made such a big fuss over her that she couldn't wait to escape his attention and go home. He and her sister-in-law, Dawn, had begged her to spend the night, but after being shot at and seeing Agent Anderson injured, she wanted her own bed.

Of course, her evening didn't end there. One she arrived home, she changed her clothes, discovering that one of her earrings was missing, and then she called Carrie.

Even with Carrie's emotional reaction, that call was easy compared to the call she had to make to her parents. Her mother sounded on the verge of swooning as only a Southern woman can. Her father demanded that she let him hire protection to watch her. She tried to explain that having armed men with her while she talked to trafficking victims wouldn't go over well. Thankfully, he didn't mention the mass grave, not that he would after receiving news that his daughter had been shot at. He did have some tact.

He kept insisting on the protection. Finally, she mentioned that she wasn't alone and told them about Agent Anderson. She explained that he might be the target, not her. Only then did her father back down. She had ended the call unsure if she would find security at her front door when she left for work. To her relief, no one but Josh waited to drive her back to the hospital parking lot to retrieve her car. After all that excitement in one night, she longed for the quiet busyness of the office.

Several people occupied the chairs in the lobby, engrossed in forms. Carrie looked up from the receptionist desk.

"Hey, boss." She sprang from her seat. "How you feeling?"

"A little sore, but okay."

Carrie grasped Savannah's hand. "Do the police know who did this?"

"I haven't heard anything yet. I'm sure they're still investigating." Savannah took a step toward her office.

"Oh." Carrie waved a message slip at her. "A Special Agent Anderson called. He said he realized he didn't give you his contact information."

"All right."

Savannah tried to take the slip but Carrie wouldn't let go. "He stressed that you could call him anytime you needed. Anytime. Is he the one who saved you?"

"Yes."

Carrie grinned. "He has a nice voice. Is he cute?"

Carrie wouldn't leave her alone if she told him how good Special Agent Anderson looked. Savannah frowned. "You can't tell how a man looks from how he sounds on the phone."

"Hmm. He's gorgeous, isn't he?"

"I'll be in my office." Savannah pulled the slip from her fingers and Carrie laughed.

"I think you should go thank him in person."

Even though she saw through Carrie's thinly veiled matchmaking attempts, going to see Agent Anderson wasn't a bad idea. Her father had probably showered the man with gifts already. Maybe she should do something, too.

Savannah turned down a hallway lined with glass front offices and oak doors. People fish tanks occupied by her staff. Her office didn't have glass walls like the others. Some cases required privacy. It also allowed her to get away from the world when she needed to reset her mind. Something she needed to do often.

A vase of lavender roses sat on the corner of her desk. She smiled, put her things down, and plucked the card from the arrangement. The roses had a unique scent. Someone must have heard about the shooting last night.

She opened the envelope and read the card.

That handwriting. All the color seemed to drain from the room and her chest constricted.

I've been thinking of you.
Miss you and hope to see you soon.
Mitch

She dropped the card on the desk as if it had scorched her fingers.

"Who are they from?" Carrie asked from behind her. Savannah jumped hard and sent the roses spinning. Carrie reacted faster than Savannah did, steadying the vase.

"You frightened me." Not as much as seeing Mitch's name on the card.

"Sorry. I just wanted to know who sent the flowers." Carrie stared at her. "Are you okay?"

Mitch sent flowers, like nothing had happened. *Not that he knows what I saw...*

Her stomach twisted in a knot.

"I'm still jittery." Her voice warbled. The card had fallen face down on the desk. Savannah picked it up and stuffed it back into the envelope.

Carrie raised an eyebrow. "So?"

"So what?"

"Who are the roses from? They're Vera Wang so they have to be from someone special."

Savannah's stomach flipped again. "Just someone from my past."

"Well, he sure knows how to make a statement," Carrie said, fingering the soft petals of the roses. "I thought they might be from Agent Anderson."

Savannah wished Agent Anderson had sent the flowers. She would be filled with joy instead of fear.

The main line rang and Carrie rushed back to her desk. Savannah immediately closed her office door before any more inquiring employees wandered in.

She flopped down in her chair. A year without so much as a phone call and now flowers. A year since she walked out of his warehouse and his life. The air in the room thickened. She pressed her face into her palms, but it didn't stop the images from flooding her mind. Each detail remained as sharp as the day they were recorded into her memory.

The buzz from the phone jolted her up from her chair.

"Savannah, did you forget your meeting today?" Carrie asked. "You should be gone."

"Mr. Ward," Savannah half-asked and half-replied. "Right. Two o'clock. Can you call him and reschedule?"

"Sure. How about tomorrow at eleven?"

"Great." Savannah noted the date on her desktop calendar.

"I'll give him a call." A slight pause. "Are you sure you're okay?"

"Yes." *That didn't sound convincing.* "Maybe it wasn't a good idea to come in today. I think I should go home."

"You should."

Savannah rose from her chair, being careful not to look at the card. Her legs wobbled as she made her way to the door. The flowers were Mitch's herald. He wouldn't be far behind. Her mind flittered to the shooting earlier. Could he have…but he didn't know. If he did, she would have to leave everything behind again.

That's right, Savannah. Run. That's what you always do. The thought sapped the rest of her energy. She flopped down in her chair, and for the first time in a year, she cried.

Chapter 4

The pain in Will's arm made the decision to stay home a no-brainer. Although, staying home brought another kind of pain. Jordan's presence permeated his small townhouse in Alexandria, VA. He'd bought the place specifically so Jordan wouldn't have to grow up without knowing what it was like to have a backyard. Now it looked like that would happen after all.

Pushing thoughts of Jordan aside, Will fixed himself a cup of coffee. He needed something to distract him. He tried cleaning but the throbbing in his arm axed that idea. He could always work on the logistics of packing up his house. Another heavy topic. His mind drifted to the house raid and the man on the lawn. *Now that's something I can do.*

He scrolled through his phone and found the number of Officer Zachary Jacobs. As usual, his ex-partner answered on the first ring. "Hey, Will. What's shakin', Bacon?"

Will laughed at his old nickname. Zach had described Will to another Baltimore officer as "lean like bacon." Will didn't consider bacon all that lean, but the name stuck. "Same ol'."

"Good to hear from you. How's the transfer prep going?"

"Slow."

"You should be an expert on transfers by now."

Will laughed. "Are you still sore about that?"

"As about as sore as I would be if someone had tried to break up Batman and Robin. Captain America and Bucky. Joker and Harley Quinn - "

"Okay, I get the point."

"You messed up a dynamic duo, but at least it was for a good cause. You needed to do right by your son."

Will swallowed. Zach didn't know the truth. He didn't want to go into that right now. "I'm calling to ask a favor."

"Shoot."

"I had a suspect who threatened me and escaped. He said he knew me from Baltimore. The problem is I don't remember him."

"Unfortunate side effect of age."

Will snorted. "Anyway, I was wondering if you could help me figure out who he is. That might help me find him."

"They still have you working cases this close to your transfer?"

"Just busywork."

"Okay, man. So what are we looking for?"

Will described the man. "The biggest clue is this man might be connected to human trafficking."

The line grew silent and Will could picture Zach leaning his elbow on the corner of his brown, standard issue desk and propping his head on his hand. "We didn't work many of those. That should narrow down the search quite a bit."

"Thanks."

"You're welcome. We have to get together before you move to the other side of the world."

"Definitely."

Will ended the call. Any info Zach came up with would help. Will rose, but as soon as he sat the cell phone down on the table, it buzzed. The caller ID read Two Rivers.

Will sucked in a breath. *Jordan's school.* "Will Anderson."

"Mr. Anderson, this is Ms. Jackson. I am calling about Jordan's project. He still hasn't turned it in yet, and I've already given him an extension."

Will gripped the phone and tried to keep anger from his tone. "Have you tried his mother?"

"I have. Several times. I haven't been able to reach her and she hasn't returned my calls." Will imagined Ms. Jackson's matronly face creased with a frown. Her deep concern for all her students impressed him. Jordan seemed to think she deserved the best teacher in the world award.

"I will give her a call but from now on, it would be best if you directed any concerns about Jordan to his mother."

"I understand. I'm sorry to trouble you. It's just that Jordan is such a good student, and I would hate to see him fail. I thought I would take a chance and call you. You're a wonderful father."

Sadness coiled around his chest. "Thank you. I'll give his mother a call."

Will ended the call and took a couple of deep breaths. He had put too much into Jordan's education for Shantel to ruin it with her irresponsibility. The project was probably something simple. He and Jordan could complete it in a couple of hours. He could find out what the project was from Ms. Jackson.

He started to dial the school, but then remembered his words to Ms. Jackson. Words he'd recited over the past two months. Shantel was now solely responsible for Jordan's needs. He needed to follow his own advice and let Shantel handle things.

Will dialed Shantel instead. He would keep his promise no matter how nerve-wracking it would be.

The phone rang three times and Will let out a growl. Shantel never answered after the third ring. How can you have a young child and not answer your phone?

Her voicemail clicked on. He had to hold the phone away from his ear as the recording started with what seemed like twenty minutes of music by Beyoncé. He'd told her to change it but like everything else, she defied him. He put the phone back to his ear just in time to catch her brief instructions to leave a message.

"Shantel, this is Will. The school called me today about Jordan's project." He clenched his jaw. "I thought we agreed that it would be best to take me off the contact information for Jordan." *This is useless.* "Call me when you get this message."

Why did she have to make things difficult?

*

The idea of going home held no appeal. Savannah got in her car but just sat. So weak. Every time she was faced with her past, she crumbled. When would she get to the point when she didn't shatter like glass? Her secrets would eventually consume her, but what could she do? Speaking up would only put her in danger. Mitch hadn't suspected anything because she'd kept her mouth shut. The less she said, the better.

Only Josh knew something happened that night and that was only because she'd gone straight to his apartment from the warehouse. She remembered his alarmed look when he saw her tear-streaked face. No matter how much he pleaded with her, she never told him what she'd seen. It was too horrible to repeat. She'd had a year's worth of nightmares to relive every single detail. Sometimes, that night amazed her. How could something as simple as dropping off sample wedding invitations to her fiancé's business turn into the worse night of her life?

She'd gone straight from work to King Sugar, the Alverez family business. Mitch ran all of the day-to-day operations.

Her first stop was his office, but she found it empty. She left the samples on his desk, but figured he was still working on shipments. He had spent a lot of time tracking shipments.

She'd wondered why that was so important that he needed to do that himself, but the mystery was solved that night. Most of the lights were out, and she only found her way by running her hand along the shelving. She got to the end of a row and prepared to call out to Mitch, but the words lodged in her throat.

Before her, on the main warehouse floor, was a horrible operation. Several large crates sat near the door and a truck was backed up to the loading bay. In another corner, a disheveled group of mostly women stood huddled together. Men worked at unloading the trailer on the back truck…unloading bodies. The men, most of them Mitch's employees, carried each corpse by their arms and legs and tossed them into large, wooden containers with an odd, swirled logo on them. Mitch stood in the corner, overseeing everything.

Savannah had stepped back into the shadows, hand pressed to her mouth to stifle a scream. No one had to explain what she was seeing. There had been rumors that King Sugar was employing illegals but this was way beyond anything she wanted to believe. Now she couldn't deny it. Mitch wasn't the person anyone thought he was, and she was engaged to him. Her reaction still baffled and horrified her.

She did nothing.

She'd quietly crept out of the warehouse and never told a soul what she'd seen.

Questions haunted her the next few days and they blurred into a confusing mess. How would she get out of her engagement to Mitch? Not the fact that Mitch was breaking the law. Not the victims. Herself and her seemingly perfect life. She worried about how her mother's socialite friends would react to the broken engagement. She had enough courage to call off the engagement, but not enough to report Mitch.

Savannah's eyes misted as her mind drifted back to the flowers sitting on her desk. They might as well be poison. She didn't grasp how dangerous Mitch was until much later, once she opened Plateau. Her mind reeled at how men like him could turn a human into currency and not bat an eye. She'd run to get away from him, but how many others wanted to run but couldn't?

A tap sounded on the window and Savannah screamed. She turned to find Carrie's confused face staring back at her, Mitch's flowers in her arms. Savannah took a few breaths and rolled the window down.

Carrie pouted. "I'm sorry. I thought you saw me."

"It's okay."

"You got a message from MPD, and then I noticed you'd left your flowers. I figured you were still here and ran out." She handed the message slip and the flowers through the window.

I just can't seem to get away from Mitch. "Thank you."

Carrie gave her a sad smile. "I promise that's the last time I'm going to scare you today."

Savannah forced a laugh. "You promise?"

The light joke was enough to soothe Carrie, and the woman went back inside. Savannah stared at the flowers. She had to get rid of them. Why didn't she just throw them away? She knew why. Carrie would ask too many questions. An idea formed in her head as she lifted the message slip. She would get rid of the flowers for good tomorrow.

The message was from Officer Dunn, urging Savannah to call as soon as she could. Savannah's heart sank as she located her cell phone and dialed the number Officer Dunn had given. She stared at the flowers while the phone rang.

"Officer Dunn."

"Good afternoon. This is Savannah Elliott. You left a message for me to call you."

"Oh, good. Glad you called back so soon."

That doesn't sound promising. "Is everything all right?"

"Unfortunately, no. We heard from one of our informants that someone ordered a hit in a parking garage and still wants the target dead."

Savannah sank in her seat. That meant this wasn't random. "Did they say who the target was?"

"No, so that means both you and Agent Anderson are still in danger. I've requested patrol cars to do routine surveillance at your job and home. It's not much, but at least it's something."

It's better than having Daddy hire protection for me. "Thank you."

"I'll keep you posted."

Savannah ended the call, stomach in knots. The police must have thought this was serious if they've ordered patrols. If Mitch was involved, it was.

*

Will finished off the last bite of catfish, which put a grin on his mother's face. Mom's brownstone had an air of calm, despite the activity of the city outside the windows. The dinners were physically and mentally refreshing.

"Wonderful as usual, Mom." He rose from the table, plate in hand, retrieved her plate, and carried them into the kitchen. "You know you don't have to feed me every week."

"I want to. Especially now."

Will scraped the fish bones in the trash. As much as he'd explained, she still didn't see how his transfer was good for Will or Jordan.

"I'll be home for holidays."

"And that's a good substitute for seeing you at least once a week?" She carried their drinking glasses into the small kitchen.

Will filled the sink with soapy water and rolled up his sleeves. He didn't want to start this discussion with Mom, not after the day he'd had. It was just as bad as the grilling she'd given him about the shooting. She'd even made him roll up his sleeve to prove it was really only a graze.

"You can come to see me anytime you want."

"I'm not sitting on a plane for hours. Not unless someone sedates me."

"You can do it, Mom. You've done more challenging things than that."

She placed the glasses into the water. "None quite as dangerous."

Will shot her a sideway glance with a sly grin on his face. "So staging a sit-in and getting dragged out by the police is not dangerous? You were practically a criminal."

She smiled at the joke they shared. Mom had been active in the Civil Rights Movement, fighting against the police and government, and her son went into law enforcement. "That was a long time ago. When I was younger and stupider."

"You mean braver, Mom."

She shrugged. "If that's what you want to call it. Besides, that was different. It was a good cause."

Will feigned a flinch. "Ouch. Your son isn't a good cause?"

"No, since he doesn't have to go. If you stayed here, I wouldn't have to fly."

Will gritted his teeth. "I already explained—"

"I know. I still don't see the need for such drastic measures. Jordan is not dead."

"It would be easier if he was," Will said before he could consider his words.

He paid for his impulsiveness. His mother whacked him across the back with an oven mitt. It barely stung, but the blow knocked him back to reality.

His mother stood beside him, hands on her hips. "Don't you ever say that again." No one would imagine how much fire this 5"4', silver haired, lovely woman possessed. Her toughness sometimes astounded Will. She'd dug in and raised Will alone after his father had died. "You don't want him dead."

"I didn't mean that. I just meant to say that it's harder to do this when he's right here in the same city and I can't see him. His school keeps calling me and I can't do anything."

"Nothing is stopping you from going over and seeing him."

"This is complicated." Will placed one of the dishes in the rack harder than he intended.

"What I know is you love that little boy, and he loves you. That's simple enough for me."

They finished the dishes in silence. It would be great to go and pick Jordan up, bring him to Nana's house and let him eat himself silly. Or take him to the park and work on his batting. Will would even enjoy working on the project the school had called about, as long as he was with Jordan. So easy to just drive to Jordan. It pained Will to think of Jordan suffering the fate he did, growing up without a father. No, not without a father, but without Will as a father.

As if she could hear Will's thoughts, Mom draped her arm around his shoulders. "Everything is going to be fine."

Will leaned his head against hers, his heart sinking. "I don't see how."

His phone chirped from his pocket. He moved away from his mother, and thankfully, the subject matter.

"Will Anderson."

"Agent Anderson, this is Officer Dunn. How's the arm?"

Will eased into one of the chairs at his mother's kitchen table. "Better."

"That's good." Her clipped words made it clear that she wasn't calling out of concerned about his arm. "I have an update on the shooting."

Will listened as she told him what he'd already feared. The shooting was an ordered hit. Had to be with such a deliberate action. Dunn told him that whoever ordered the hit still wanted either he or Savannah dead. He clinched his fist as she told him they hadn't figured out who was behind the shooting or whether he was the target.

"I would think it would be you," Officer Dunn said. "But we can't rule out Ms. Elliott."

"Have you gotten patrols for Ms. Elliott?"

"Yes, and I think you should have some, too. Since you're FBI, I figured you could ask your people to keep an eye on you. That would allow me to use all my resources on Ms. Elliott."

Smart thinking. "I'll talk to my boss."

"Good. Stay safe."

Will returned the phone to his pocket and pinched the end of his nose. Either scenario, Will as the target or Savannah as the target, was pretty serious. Serious since someone had ordered a hit on Savannah with so many witnesses around or that hit was aimed at him, an FBI agent.

Mom took the seat across from him. "What happened?"

Will told her the latest developments and instead of fear, Will watched his mother's face harden for a fight. He reached out and grasped her hand. "Between the FBI and MPD, we'll figure out who's behind this."

She scowled, but then rose and gave him a hug. He accepted, fighting back the heaviness creeping in on him. He'd been so concerned about saying goodbye to Jordan that he'd overlooked that he would have to say goodbye to his mother, too.

As if she could read his thoughts, she said, "I'll miss you, too."

Chapter 5

Savannah gripped the vase of roses in one hand and pressed the elevator button with the other. The movement of the closing door fanned a burst of fragrance into the air. She imagined the flowers weren't from Mitch and inhaled deep.

But they were from Mitch. All night, she'd toyed with throwing them in the trash as they sat on her dining room table, but giving them to Marisol was a better idea. The poor girl deserved some beauty in her life. Why not use the flowers to bring some color to her room? Hopefully, Mitch would never know.

The thought of Mitch returning to her life set her knees wobbling as she walked down the hall to the nurse's station. One of the nurses who'd been on duty the day before looked up from the computer screen and smiled.

"What pretty flowers."

"They are for Marisol Benitez." Savannah flashed the ID MPD had given her so she could have access to hospitalized victims.

"Oh." The nurse frowned. "Marisol was moved to ICU this morning. Kidney infection. I don't think she's allowed visitors at this point."

Savannah blew out a puff of air. How much more could this girl take? "Are they going to bring her back to her bed here?"

"Don't know yet." The nurse grinned and extended her hands. "If you want, I can keep the roses here until her doctor decides what he's going to do."

Savannah slid the vase across the counter. "Thank you." Marisol may not get to see them before they wilted, but at least someone would enjoy them.

"How are the other victims?"

The nurse flipped a chart. "No change in their conditions."

Savannah's heart sank. Most of the cases she assisted involved girls well enough to at least identify themselves. The deplorable conditions in the house made it a perfect breeding ground for disease. All the girls had severe upper respiratory problems and were under heavy medication to combat it. Sadly, this was only the beginning of their long health battle. Savannah whispered a prayer. Their recovery was the first step to rebuilding their lives. She was anxious to see it begin.

*

Two items sat in the middle of Will's desk: a manila envelope and a phone slip. He picked up the phone slip first. Officer Grant. Not someone he wanted to talk to after the emotional night he'd had with his mother.

Will grunted and placed the slip near his phone. The envelope was from MPD, probably information from the crime scene investigation.

This calls for coffee.

As a matter of fact, the whole morning so far called for coffee. Not even the stark white walls of the office were enough to jar his brain to alertness. Shantel hadn't called last night, not that he expected her to, but he stayed up late waiting anyway. Will had long suspected that she screened his calls and intentionally waited days to call him back. Unfortunately, the extension for Jordan's project would have long passed.

Agent Carter passed him in the hallway on the way to the break room with a cup of coffee in hand. "I didn't expect to see you today."

"Figured I'd come in and help find the suspect who got away."

Agent Carter nodded. "Or the guys who shot at you. If we knew for sure you were targeted, I could take over the case."

I wish someone would take over all my cases.

"I did manage to keep the news agencies in the dark about your involvement in the shooting. Not information we want released to the public." Carter sipped his coffee. "Any more updates on the raid? Have they located our suspect?"

"Not yet. MPD sent over some evidence. I'll start working on it as soon as I get some coffee."

Carter smiled and continued down the hallway. "You're a great agent. I'm sure you'll find that suspect in no time."

Will grimaced. He shouldn't get too involved in this case. He might have to move in the middle of it. He carried his cup of coffee back to his desk and turned his focus to the papers in the envelope.

Unfortunately, Will had reached his maximum allowed cups of coffee by 11am. Processing the information from MPD had been an exercise in futility. He flipped through the pictures of the crime scene and shook his head. Litter covered the floor. Sadly, too much evidence could be just as bad as not enough. Sorting through a scene like this required divine guidance to determine what would help catch the suspect and what was trash. If the guys who ran the house were careful enough, there probably wasn't anything useful for the squad. But that didn't mean that Will didn't have to go through it all.

He sat the photos aside and picked up a stack of papers. The stapled packet appeared to be a listing of make, model and tag numbers of cars, but there was nothing to tell him why it had been included. Will grunted. Guess he couldn't avoid Officer Grant any longer.

Will skipped the pleasantries when Officer Grant answered the phone. "This is Agent Anderson. I got your package. I'm calling about the ledger included."

"Yeah. Apparently, our tipster is a member of the Neighborhood Watch. When the foot traffic to the house picked up, he started recording the tags of the cars he saw over there."

You could have put that on note. "That was good thinking."

"The list goes back six months. We haven't started tracking down the cars yet. Probably all customers, but I thought you might turn up something useful."

Will clinched his jaw. Now MPD was giving him busywork.

"We interviewed one of the guys we took into custody from the brothel. He was pretty much useless," Officer Grant continued. "He's been going to the house for a year and didn't remember much of anything except his favorite girl was gone and that he had a new girl."

Will gripped the phone, pushing back the inherent disgust that came with this line of work. "Okay, thanks."

"I've also got another suspect you might be interested in talking to. He's being tight-lipped. Maybe you can loosen it."

Will rolled his shoulders. More busywork. "Sure."

"See you tonight."

Will massaged his temples. The ledger sat in front of him. Going through it would be hours of manpower. Hours he didn't have if he was going to the interview tonight.

His desk phone rang.

"Will Anderson."

The nasally voice of the receptionist at the visitor center greeted him. "Agent Anderson. You have a visitor. A Savannah Elliott."

Will's fingers halted. "I'll be right down."

Fighting to keep his nerves calm, Will took the elevator down to the lobby. All his fighting evaporated when he saw her standing near the visitor's desk in a rich blue suit. Her hair held less curl than the last time he'd seen it but still held all of its soft movement. It did a soft swish when she turned to face him.

Her smile grew as he approached, sending tendrils of warmth down to his toes. "Good morning." She tucked her hair behind her ear, a faint pink tint on her cheeks. "I should have called first."

Wow. "It's all right. You came at a good time."

"So that means you can have a quick cup of coffee with me?"

His mind floated to the cups of coffee he'd had earlier. One more wouldn't hurt. "Of course."

He led her to the small café housed in the building and they ordered. Will kept his professional demeanor in place. No time to daydream about what it would be like to have coffee with her in a non-professional setting.

Savannah chose a table near the wall and they sat. "How is your arm?"

"Better."

She smiled. "I'm so glad to hear that. I was worried about you."

"No need."

"You saved my life. I've earned the right to worry about you." She reached into her purse. "I have something for you. A gift from me and my family."

Will held up his hands. "That's not necessary."

Savannah quirked an eyebrow. "It's this or my father, the governor of Georgia, is going to thank you in a very public way. Trust me, you don't want that."

Will's jaw fell open, but he managed to close it quickly. A governor's daughter. *That explains her poise.* "I'll take your word for it."

She slid a small envelope across the table. Will opened it, found a gift card for a very high end men's clothing store and laughed.

Savannah grinned brightly. "We figured the least we could do is replace your suit."

He stuck the gift card in his pocket. "Thank you."

"You're very welcome, and that should keep Daddy off your back."

"Sounds like two gifts in one."

She gave him an exaggerated nod. "It is."

Will turned his cup in his hands. A casual conversation would be great here, but he literally didn't have time for it. Not with the transfer looming. Clearly, he was attracted to Savannah. What man wouldn't be? One good conversation, however, would be all his heart needed to move forward.

Savannah took a sip of her coffee and sighed. "I went to the hospital today to check on Marisol. She's been moved to ICU for a kidney infection."

Will pinched the bridge of his nose. Victims who were willing to talk were valuable resources for shutting down entire operations. Besides, he really wanted Marisol to go home alive. "Sorry to hear that."

"I've asked the doctors to keep me posted. I'll call you as soon as I hear anything."

"I appreciate that."

She paused again and then stood. "Well, I need to go. My receptionist has been worried sick about me since the shooting. I'm surprised she hasn't called yet."

As if on cue, Savannah's phone rang. She laughed.

Will stood. "You better talk to her before she calls in a missing person report."

"Right."

They walked to the front door in silence. Just before going out, she turned to face him. "Thanks again." She enveloped him in a quick hug, and before he could wrap his arms around her, she breezed away and out the door.

Will let out a sigh loud enough to catch the attention of other agents walking past him. He headed to the elevator bank, determined to still his emotions before he got back to his desk.

He failed.

He flopped down in his chair and focused on the evidence from Officer Grant. That should help dislodge the smell of Savannah's hair from his thoughts. Will logged into the DMV system and while he waited, he slid the ledger in front of him again. Black Honda, gray station wagon, white box truck, blue minivan. Whoever wrote it was pretty thorough. He flipped to the second page. *It would take the rest of my time in DC to hunt down all these vehicles.*

His eyes stopped on another listing for a white box truck.

He turned back to the first page, found the listing for the white box truck on that page. The license plates were the same.

Hope flittered through him. *Finally. A lead.* Over the years, he'd seen victims transported in everything from freight containers to car trunks. The preferred method was large vehicles like box trucks, most outfitted with false bottom floors.

He keyed the tag number in and the results of his searched popped onto the screen.

The truck was registered to a Juan Valdez. Will smirked. Most likely an alias. The address was local. Will enlarged the picture on Juan's driver's license and sighed. Not the man from the house. That would have made things easier. So who was Juan and how did he fit into the brothel's puzzle?

*

Footsteps in the hallway caught her attention. The office had remained quiet since she arrived from her meeting with Will. She'd hoped for some sort of distraction, but the quiet gave her all she needed to rehash their short coffee break...and the hug. She nearly groaned each time she thought of it. Why had she hugged him?

She looked up to find her brother standing in her doorway grinning. "There's my professional, successful sister."

Savannah stood and hugged him. "Were we supposed to have lunch today?"

Joshua sat in the leather armchair in front of her desk. "Nope. Just doing big brother duty." He glanced around her office. "So how are you? Any developments on the shooting?"

"MPD is still working on it. They've made a little progress."

Joshua leaned forward. "Have they caught someone?"

She shook her head. "According to their sources, whoever ordered the hit still wants it carried out."

He frowned. "I think you should have taken daddy's offer for hired protection."

Savannah sighed. "Don't forget I may not be the target. Besides, the police have started patrols here and at my condo."

"It's not too late to take Daddy up -"

"I can't have armed men following me around. I'm sure MPD will do a wonderful job."

He folded his hands in his lap, and then unfolded them again, and then picked invisible lint from his slacks.

Savannah cocked her head to the side and studied him. "What did you do, Joshua?"

"Why do you think I did something?" His voice rose a little too high for him to be innocent. His brow furrowed, a familiar expression. She and Joshua could pass for twins despite the three-year age difference in Joshua's favor. She would have worn the same furrow if she'd done something he wasn't happy about.

"Your face and this nice, but unplanned visit."

63

Joshua sighed. "Mitch called my house yesterday, and Dawn told him all your information before I figured out who was on the phone."

Savannah folded her hands in front of her on her desk to hide the shudder that ran through her. "That explains it."

"Explains what?" Josh's eyes filled with concern.

"He sent me flowers."

"I'm sorry, Anna." Josh leaned forward and grasped her hands. "Dawn doesn't know him. I'll make sure she knows not to give anyone else information about you."

"It's not like finding me is that difficult."

"Someday you're going to tell me the whole story about what happened between you and Mitch."

"Things didn't work out. That's all." Savannah focused her attention on her desk. She had managed to keep her mouth shut this long about that night. She wasn't about to start talking now. It stung that she couldn't tell Josh, one of the closest people to her, but she didn't know how to tell him or when.

"It's more to it than that. I remember how scared you were that night you showed up at my apartment—"

Savannah held up her hand. "Do we have to discuss this? I'm still recovering from the flowers."

Joshua glanced around her office. "Have I told you how proud I am of you starting this place?"

Savannah remembered the day she told Joshua and Dawn about her plan to take advantage of their father's political connections and become a human rights activist. They had been baffled by her decision, not knowing her real reason for starting the organization, but remained great cheerleaders. Their encouragement got her through a rough first year.

Savannah grinned. "Only a million times."

Joshua's encouragement and support took on more a fatherly tone at times. Although their father used his connections to help Plateau grow faster than most start-ups, he never offered his praise. His influence as a governor opened many doors that she wouldn't have been able to pry open. If he hadn't put in a word for her at Metro police, she doubted anyone would have known her well enough to seek her out for the position on the Human Trafficking Taskforce. She was thankful for all he'd done despite his motives, but Joshua was the one cheering her on. Without Joshua, Savannah would still be drowning in grief and confusion.

"Thanks for coming by to tell me about Mitch's phone call."

"That wasn't the only reason why I stopped by."

Savannah took a sip of her coffee. "What? You didn't come by to shower me with compliments?"

Joshua took a deep breath. "Mama is coming to visit."

Savannah held her cup suspended above her desk. "When?"

"This weekend." Easter weekends were big deals in the Elliott family. Even when their parents couldn't join them, Joshua, Dawn and Savannah had made it a point to have Easter dinner together. It had been years since they spent Easter, or any other holiday for that matter, with their mother, Esther Elliott. The distance had provided a nice buffer, so much so that Savannah had forgotten most of her mother's rules for appropriate behavior.

"Apparently, Dad has business in DC next week. She decided to come up a little early to spend Easter with us." Joshua grinned. "And she's cooking Easter dinner."

"How did you manage that?"

Joshua lowered his voice and winked. "I worked my charms on her but if I tell you how, I'll have to kill you."

Savannah laughed. "You've got skills." Southern cooking ranked at the top of Savannah's list of things she missed about Georgia. Dawn was a great substitute but Dawn and Savannah's culinary ability paled in comparison to the real thing. A rare treat since her mother had all but stopped cooking when she was thrust into the public spotlight. Unfortunately, Mama's cooking would be the only, small bright spot in the whole weekend. Being in the same state with her already began to jar Savannah's nerves.

A soft knock on the door diverted her attention. Carrie stood with a slightly amazed look on her face.

"Sorry to interrupt, Boss, but Megan Ross, the associate producer of BET News called. She wants to interview you about the mass grave in Georgia."

Savannah glanced at Josh, who wore the same amazed expression Carrie did. "Are you serious?"

Carrie leaned on the doorframe. "She wants to know if you would be available this evening for an interview at the studio on 9th street."

"Call her back, tell her yes and see if you can get a list of questions."

Carrie rushed from the room.

Media attention was a mixed bag. On the one hand, it was a great opportunity for Savannah to bring awareness to human trafficking. BET would reach more people in one broadcast than a mouth of her stumping at community outreaches and town meetings. She had gone to forum after forum explaining the work Plateau did. This interview would broaden her voice. On the other, especially when a big news story broke, it could make Savannah seem opportunistic. She would have to tailor her interview with the soberness it deserved.

"Congratulations, Baby Sis." Joshua stood and smoothed the creases in his slacks. "I guess that's my cue to go. We'll have a little dinner on Friday once Mama arrives. It will be nice. You'll see."

I doubt it. "Do you need me to bring something?"

"I think Dawn has everything sorted but you can call her and ask. I'm staying out of her and Mama's way. I'm only in it for the eats." He waved goodbye and blew her a kiss. When he was out of sight, Savannah stared at the papers on her desk, not really seeing them. Her life had been quiet. What's with all the complications now?

*

Will parked his car outside the DC lockup. Even in the afternoon sun, the building seemed to be shaded in gray. Was the depressing look of law enforcement buildings supposed to be a deterrent? Or was it so grimy to mirror the hopelessness of those incarcerated inside? Either way, Will took his time climbing the stairs.

The desk sergeant directed him to Officer Grant's cube.

"You're here." Officer Grant stood and closed the folder in front of him. "Let's get this done."

Will smirked. Officer Grant's desk looked like Will's had a month ago.

Their trip to interrogation led them through another squad room much louder than Will's. Not an unpleasant din. That meant people were working and criminals were being caught.

Officer Grant stopped outside the door. "Do you want me to sit in?"

Will bit back a smile. Time to show him the difference between interrogating suspects and victims. "Sure."

Once Officer Grant swung the door open, Will quickly cataloged the tiny room. A table, four chairs, and one very nervous man in an orange jumpsuit. Just the way Will liked. The suspect, Greg Rawls, eyed Will suspiciously but glared at Officer Grant. Hmm. Will's mind began planning how to work Rawls' dislike for Grant to their advantage.

"This is Special Agent Anderson from the FBI." Grant sat in the chair closest to the wall. Will took the seat directly in front of Rawls and put the folder in his hand down on the table.

"I dunno why you got me in here. I told you everything I know." Rawls sniffled and rubbed his hand over his knotty hair.

"You look like a man who can tell everything he knows in one interview," Will said, locking gazes with Rawls.

"You tryin' to say I'm dumb?"

Will crossed his legs. "You can't be very smart to withhold information that could help us catch the guys holding those girls."

Rawls leaned back in his chair and threw his arms up. "I don't know nothing 'bout what was going on in there."

Officer Grant opened his mouth to speak, but Will tapped the table with his fingertip. "I think you know more than you're telling." Will opened the folder and pulled out a picture of Juan Valdez and slid it across to Rawls. "Who's this?"

Rawls looked genuinely confused. "I dunno."

Will let out a sigh. "You're not being wise. I know you know him."

"Nah, man. Never seen him in the house before."

"He was in there on several occasions."

Rawls pointed to the picture. "This man ain't never set foot in that house."

Will folded his arms. "Let me explain a little something to you, Greg. Helping me has its benefits. I could possibly put in a good word for you. If you don't, I'll have to leave you in the wonderful company of Officer Grant."

Right on cue, Grant offered Rawls a too-bright smile. Will suppressed his own grin.

"Come on! I'm telling the truth."

Will snatched the picture up and held it in front of Rawls' face. "His truck was parked outside the house once every three weeks. How could you not see him?"

Rawls laid his head down on the table. "Lotta trucks come and go. I didn't take note of all of 'em."

"This one would have been hard to miss. Big white box truck."

Rawls stiffened. "Hold on, hold on. That's not him."

Officer Grant's eyebrow quirked. "What do you mean?"

"That's not the guy who drove the white box truck. Don't look nothin' like him."

Will sat back. "Then what does he look like?"

Distress filled his eyes. "Look, man. If I tell you what he looked like, could you put me somewhere other than here with him?" He tipped his head in Grant's direction.

Grant leaned forward. "I love you, too, sweetheart."

Rawls sent Will an incredulous look.

"I'll do my best."

Rawls took a deep breath and leaned back. "He was Hispanic or Latino...whatever they are callin' themselves now. He had an earring in his ear, and dude was tatted up. Whole right arm."

Will schooled his face. *The man from the yard.* "Can you describe him to a sketch artist?"

"Yeah, yeah. I saw him real good. He…" Rawls stopped and made a face that reminded Will of Jordan's expression when he got caught doing wrong.

Will raised an eyebrow. "He what?"

Rawls let out a deep breath. "He was the dude who collected payments and brought in the drugs and girls."

Will gave Officer Grant an amused look. "Well, look at that. He does know something."

Officer Grant didn't seem to be offended by the revelation but it had to sting. It would have if it had been Will's suspect.

"Look, dude is scary."

Will rose from the chair. "I'll send in a sketch artist. Until then, I'll have to leave you in Officer Grant's capable hands."

Rawls let out a groan and Will exited behind Grant.

Grant folded his arms. "I'll set up the sketch artist for tomorrow."

Will nodded. "Thanks for the assist in there."

Grant's face hardened. "Yeah, good job."

Will held his smirk until he got to his car.

Chapter 6

Will's mother had gotten him hooked on morning news. News and his obvious coffee addiction. Before he purchased his own place, they would begin their day together with a cup of gourmet brew and the news. While they sipped, they would watch the newscasts from several channels, each one giving a slightly different perspective on the stories they presented. Black Entertainment Television ranked at the top of his mother's list of favorites. Will formed a habit of watching it, too, even though it wasn't his preference. Their stories held a certain relevance to the movers and shakers in the African-American community. Mom thrived on it since she'd never really retired from being a civil rights activist.

Will stood at his mirror and fixed the knot in his tie. That done, he completed another ritual: Putting a picture of Jordan in his suit jacket. He'd started putting pictures in his jacket after he'd worked a particularly difficult case involving children. He thought of the picture as an anchor, keeping him balanced when things got rough at work. It was a reminder that there was still innocence and joy in the world. Despite the fact that he couldn't see Jordan anymore, he could still use the reminder everyday.

When his gaze returned to the TV, he saw a familiar face on the screen.

Savannah Elliott.

"This discovery shows how difficult and challenging it is to present a solid number on how many people are trafficked into the United States each year. Graves are hidden and victims are kept isolated from the rest of the world. Unfortunately, the public hasn't been adequately trained how to identify trafficked people."

Will marveled at how completely comfortable she looked being on TV. Her hair fell over her shoulders, straight and full of body. The studio lights added a rich glow to her eyes.

"What made you choose human rights as a career?" the host, Megan Ross, asked. "Did your father have a hand in your decision?"

Savannah tensed ever so slightly, and then smiled. "In a way, human rights chose me. Serving as my father's spokeswoman on the juvenile AIDS epidemic opened my eyes to the massive problem of human trafficking. Once you see that kind of depravity, you can't look away and go back to life as usual."

Will stepped closer to the TV.

Megan smiled. "Tell me about Plateau."

Savannah shifted in her seat, slightly leaning forward. "Plateau means wide open space. I thought that was a fitting title for what we do. Our job is to help victims of human trafficking restart their lives and shepherd them through the judicial system. Victims don't have anyone to fight for their rights since they are in the country illegally. We ensure that they are handled in the most humane way possible."

Will realized that he'd been standing frozen, his admiration for Savannah swelling. She knew her job and from what he'd seen in the hospital room, she did it well. Even more amazing was her choice to work in human rights. Will had chosen the job at the FBI just to get out of Baltimore. He got paid to care about the victims and Savannah did it on her own accord.

Megan's voice brought Will's attention back to the program. "The fundraiser is Saturday, April 27th at seven pm at the Gaylord at the National Harbor. Where can viewers get tickets?"

Savannah's smile stirred something in him, something he couldn't quite name at the moment. "Tickets can be purchased through my office. But if viewers can't attend the event, monetary donations are welcome and will go a long way to helping victims with services they so desperately need."

Will flipped off the TV, his mind counting his remaining days. He would still be in DC for the gala. He grabbed his cell phone and wallet, fishing out Savannah's card.

He dialed and the call went to voicemail. He frowned. It was barely seven o'clock. Who would be at the office so early? The tone sounded for him to leave a message.

"Ms. Elliott, this is Special Agent Will Anderson. Could you give me a call at your earliest convenience? Thank you."

He ended the call. She would probably get the message first thing this morning. An image of her surfaced in his thoughts, her eyes sparkling and her hair flowing over her shoulders. What an intriguing woman.

He smiled, and bounded down to the kitchen. He could stop by her office at some point in the day. His schedule would definitely allow it. He opened the refrigerator and caught a glimpse of the calendar Jordan had made for him. His stomach churned. Less than sixty days left until his transfer. Not enough time to have his attention captured by a woman.

*

The intercom on Savannah's desk phone squeaked. "Savannah, your father is on line three."

And it begins.

Even though she had anticipated the call, she still hesitated to pick it up. Talking to Daddy was a different kind of challenge than talking to Mama.

"Hi, princess."

Savannah smirked. He must have a visitor in his office. His use of her fake pet name was purely for their benefit. "Hi, Daddy."

Her father's voice filled her ear. "How are you? Any progress on the shooting case?"

"Nothing yet."

"I still think you should let me hire some protection for you."

How many times would she have to explain she didn't want his protection? "The police are doing a fine job."

"You've created quite a buzz down here with your fundraiser."

Savannah nearly laughed at his quick change of subject. Her father cared, but only in small time increments. "Great. You're still coming, right?" Her father had RSVP'd months ago, but that didn't mean something more important wouldn't prevent him from attending.

"Of course, of course. I want to be there to support my daughter."

"I appreciate that." If Daddy came, then his deep-pocketed friends would follow and she needed every dime she could get. Fighting human trafficking was like dipping the ocean out with a teaspoon and resources were used up quickly.

"I'm calling for another reason. I was hoping you could help me with something." He cleared his throat. "I'm sure you've heard about the incident in Ware County."

"I did."

"The police are pretty certain it's human trafficking. The Arizona's states attorney is still raving about how helpful you were to him. I'm sure you wouldn't mind helping out your daddy since this is your area of expertise."

Savannah stifled a sigh. Helping victims was her area of expertise, not investigating. She'd only helped States Attorney Ken Quest with an investigation because she was young and needed some experience under her belt. Not to mention she would be working with her father.

"I'm pretty busy right now, Daddy."

"It would only be a little consulting." Daddy's politician voice had always impressed her in a stomach-churning way. It reminded her of the siren's song she read in fairy tales as a child, beckoning people to their deaths with such a melodious sound. "You could give the police pointers to help find the people behind this horrible crime. I'm sure the consultant fee would help."

Leave it to Daddy to throw money at every problem. She swallowed. The money would help. "I'm not sure how much I can help."

"I would appreciate anything you're able to do."

"All right."

"Great. I'll have Denton update you on what we have. Talk to you later."

Savannah sat the receiver back on the base hoping this little project didn't take over her life.

*

Will's phone chirped. He checked the caller ID.

Shantel.

All the warm feelings from seeing Savannah on TV this morning evaporated. He gritted his teeth, sucking in a breath. At least she called back. "Will Anderson."

"I got all your messages, okay?"

Will unclenched his jaw. "Thank you for calling me back."

"Don't thank me. I don't need you thanking me or telling me what to do."

Will swiped his hand over his face. This was the parent Jordan was stuck with. "I didn't tell you what to do. I only informed you to call the school…"

"Don't you think I know what to do?"

Will gripped the phone. "Sometimes I wonder. You still haven't removed me from the emergency contact list."

She huffed. "See, this is what I get for trying to be nice."

How could one person drive him so crazy? "How is this being nice?"

"You know what? Fine. I'll take you off the list. Then you won't be able to be in Jordan's life at all."

Anger exploded in Will's chest. "Don't give me that, Shantel. You're the one who demanded that I distance myself from Jordan. You need to make up your mind. This isn't nice to me or Jordan."

"You wonder why I don't return your calls." The phone went dead.

Will stared at the phone for a moment, and then tossed it down hard enough that it skidded across his desk. No matter how much he loathed transferring halfway across the country, Shantel kept proving that it was the best decision. Then he wouldn't be jerked around by her anymore. No one deserved this kind of treatment, especially when his only fault was loving a little boy like a son.

How nice it would be to have a civil conversation with Shantel for once. He let out a huff. That wasn't going to happen, not that he remembered it ever happening even when they were dating. What had he seen in her? Not a fair question to pose to his present self. He was a very different person than he was then. Back then, civil conversations with a woman weren't as important as they were now.

He picked up his phone to return it to its holster but paused. He could call Savannah. Of course, he would use the tickets to her gala as an excuse, but he could have a civil conversation with her. That would definitely improve his mood. He grunted and shoved the phone into its case. Talking to Savannah was a temporary fix. He couldn't get accustomed to that.

He turned his attention back to the ledger. Until the sketch came back from Rawls, or another lead materialized, this was his next best shot of finding Juan. He logged back into DMV for the address listed on Juan's driver's license. Maybe it was time to pay Juan a visit.

Will read the address, 5200 Glover Road NW, Washington, DC 20015. He read it again. That address seemed familiar, like he'd been there before. He glanced at the picture of Jordan and his memory cleared. That address was to the Rock Creek Park Nature Center and Planetarium. He and Jordan had gone one weekend last year. Will growled. Seems like someone at DMV would have noticed that Juan had given the address of Rock Creek Park as his residence. Now he was back to square one.

His desk phone rang.

He snatched the receiver from the base. "Will Anderson."

"Hello, Agent Anderson." Officer Dunn's voice, though low, grated his nerves even more. "Have I called at a bad time? You sound frustrated."

Will gripped the phone and calmed his tone. "I'm working on a challenging case."

"I understand. This shooting case isn't going anywhere." He heard papers shuffle in the background. "I was wondering if you could come in tonight and look at some mug shots. I'm having Ms. Elliott come in, too."

Will rubbed his face. He would get to talk to Savannah today after all. "Of course."

*

The day had turned cool by the time Savannah pulled into the police station's parking garage.

Despite the time, the DC streets around her still buzzed with traffic. Her mind felt a little like the maze of crowded streets around her. Her thoughts zipped in multiple directions, all of them seeming to converge on her nerves.

Her mother should be at Josh's house by now. That thought pulled another: her daddy and his case. Why hadn't she told him no? Working with family would be challenging for anyone, but working with Daddy ramped up the issues. James Elliott had not become the governor of Georgia by being passive. He was a force of nature. She'd found that fascinating as a child, but now, she realized that wasn't an admirable trait. The investigation of the mass grave case fell beyond her area of expertise, but that wasn't Daddy's first concern.

Like she needed another case. She had a bundle of them at work, including Marisol, and the shooting. At least there was some hope of resolving the later if she recognized someone in the mug shots Officer Dunn put together. She pulled her coat closed and went inside. She approached the desk sergeant and gave him her name. He confirmed she was there to meet with Officer Dunn and then directed her toward the seats that lined the wall. When she turned, she spotted a familiar face.

Agent Anderson.

He sat in one of the chairs twirling something in his hand. When she stepped in his direction, he looked up, smiled and rose. Even though he stood with his weight resting on one leg, she still had to crane her neck to make eye contact.

"Savannah. You look nice."

She looked down at the gray suit she wore. Nothing special, but his complement made it feel special. Made her feel special. "I didn't realize we would be here at the same time."

He held out his hand and her diamond studded hoop earring sparkled in his palm. "I have something that belongs to you."

She grinned and took it from his hand. "I was wondering where this had gone."

"You lost it the night of the shooting. I forgot to give it to you the last time I saw you."

Savannah dropped the earring in her purse. *This man's thoughtfulness ran deep.* "Thank you."

He motioned for her to sit and then took the seat beside her. He inhaled deeply. "I saw you on BET this morning. I called your office about the fundraiser."

She shifted in her chair to face him. "How did I do? I was so nervous."

"You did great." He reached out like he would touch her arm, but then diverted his hand to the arm of her chair. She fought the urge to encourage him to follow his impulse. "It was also very informative. You've been at this a long time."

Savannah shifted in the chair to face him. "Since I was a teen. I had no idea where all my activist work and all those Spanish lessons would lead me."

"If there are any tickets left to the gala, I'd like to get two."

Savannah pasted on a smile. *Two?* "Sure. What's your girlfriend's name?" As soon as the words were out of her mouth, regret slammed her. She already suspected he was single. She'd only asked to confirm it, but she should have waited for him to offer that information.

If he saw through her ploy, he didn't let on. "I don't have a girlfriend. I'm bringing my mother."

Savannah held in a sigh. "Oh. I need her name for the place cards."

"Denise Anderson."

That name sounded familiar. "Wait. The Denise Anderson, the civil rights activist?"

Will grinned. "The one and only. You get cool points for knowing who she is."

His mother was a civil rights activist. That explained some of his grace with handling Marisol. "How can I not? I've always admired her tenacity. As a matter of fact, I'll give you your tickets for free if I can meet her."

Will chuckled. "I'll arrange for you to meet her, but I'll pay full price for both tickets. And you must call me Will."

"Deal. On both points."

"Mom and I have dinner together every Tuesday. I'm sure she wouldn't mind if you joined us next week."

Savannah bit her lip. Dinner with Will? No, dinner with Denise Anderson. "That's sounds great. I can't wait to meet her."

"I'm sure she'll be equally excited. She lives in Northeast. Do you need me to pick you up?"

"No." Savannah's voice squeaked. "I'll probably come straight from work."

"All right." He pulled out a notepad from his pocket and scribbled an address on a piece of paper. "Be there about 6:30 pm. Mom is a stickler about eating on time."

Savannah gave him a grave nod. "I understand."

Will leaned closer and her heart hammered again. He opened his mouth to speak, but Officer Dunn arrived just as he did.

Officer Dunn looked from Savannah to Will and back again. "Sorry to interrupt, but Ms. Elliott, if you're ready, you can come back to my desk."

Savannah rose. "I'll see you, Tuesday, then."

Will nodded.

Savannah followed Officer Dunn acutely aware that Will was watching her, but she dared not turn. Officer Dunn led her to a cubicle near the center of the bull pin with an odd smile on her face. When they reached the desk, Officer Dunn offered her a seat. "Are you and Agent Anderson an item?"

Savannah felt a hot blush on her cheeks. "No."

"I thought you were since he's been here for an hour waiting for you."

Savannah glanced back in the direction of waiting area. "He has?"

Officer Dunn chuckled. "Yes. And he's still here."

Could he be interested? "He's a very nice man."

Officer Dunn shuffled the papers on her desk, not looking at Savannah. "He is."

Unfortunately, Officer Dunn's comment had sent her thoughts spinning. She fought to get her focus back on what she'd come to do. In the end, she didn't need it.

Officer Dunn shuffled three pages of suspects' photos in front of her. She looked at each face, trying to recall one of them but failed. Not that she'd had high hopes. Will had shoved her to the ground so fast that night that she barely had time to process what was happening…but he had found her earring.

Savannah handed the mug shot sheets back to Officer Dunn. "I'm sorry I couldn't be more help."

Officer Dunn shrugged. "I knew this was a long shot anyway."

Savannah collected her things and Officer Dunn led her out to where Will sat… still waiting. Savannah fought her surprise but warmed at the sight of him. Maybe he was interested.

*

Will noted Savannah's surprised expression. *You shouldn't have waited, Anderson.* He rose and cleared his throat. "All done?"

Officer Dunn smirked. "She's all yours."

Savannah's eyes widened. What had they been talking about?

Savannah fell into step beside him. "That was quick. I'll walk you to your car."

Savannah laughed, the sound dancing across his emotions in a both delightful and frightening way. "Bad things happen when you walk me to my car."

Will straightened his shoulders. "Which is why I should walk you."

They navigated down to the parking lot in silence. What could he say? He was playing a dangerous game. He couldn't afford to develop feelings for Savannah, not with his pending transfer ever present. He should keep a distance. He made small talk, but even small talk with Savannah felt meaningful.

The parking garage wasn't as dark as the hospital parking lot and the lanes sloped down toward the exit. "Where is your car?"

She laughed. "That sounds familiar." She pointed down the aisle and froze.

Police lights flashed at the end of the row. He glanced at Savannah, noting the confused look on her face. "Is your car down there?"

He almost didn't have to ask. Her expression told him he was right. Her look of discomfort increased with each step.

Will hadn't seen Savannah's car that night, but he remembered she'd said it was silver. The officers were gathered around a small silver car. Savannah let out a gasp when she spotted it.

Will fished his badge out of his pocket and flashed it to the first officer that passed. "What's going on?"

The officer glanced at his badge. "Break-in."

Savannah trembled. "I think that's my car."

The officer asked for her tag number and driver's license. After studying her license for a moment, the officer shook his head. "I'm sorry, ma'am."

Savannah swayed and Will grasped her hand.

The officer ushered her forward. "Can you answer some questions for us?"

Savannah nodded and Will expected her to release his hand, but she didn't. An ache formed in his chest for her. How many times was this woman going to be questioned by the police in one week? Sadly, Will has some questions of his own. This was too much of a coincidence. First the shooting, now this. Savannah was probably the target of shooting. How else could he explain this brazen attempt to vandalize her car in a police parking lot?

He flipped out his phone and texted Officer Dunn. She needed to be here. It would be easier if one officer was handling all the cases. Officer Dunn appeared at the scene within five minutes moving faster than he'd seen her move since the night of the shooting.

She stepped next to Will. "Are you thinking what I'm thinking?"

"That Savannah must be the target?"

Officer Dunn nodded. "I'll increase her patrols."

"Good idea."

Savannah returned to Will's side paler than she'd been when she left. Will placed his hand on her shoulder and her bottom lip trembled. Before he could blink, tears started streaming down her cheeks. On impulse, Will pulled her to him and she came into his arms without resistance.

"I'll take you home."

Savannah sniffled. "I can call my brother." She pulled away slightly, and the emptiness of her absence weighed on his shoulders. She dug her phone from her purse. Will tried not to listen to her conversation, but standing so close he couldn't help be hear.

Savannah dropped her head. "Oh, right. I forgot." She paused. "No. I'll be okay."

She ended her call. She swiped her hand across her cheek. "Will, I'm sorry but I will need that ride after all. Would you mind taking me to my brother's house? He lives in Maryland. Upper Marlboro. I understand if you can't drive me all the way out there…"

Will extended his crooked arm to her before she finished speaking. "I'll drive you."

She slipped her arm around his and he led her to his car. *Officer Dunn needed to make some progress on this case before someone finishes the job.*

Savannah said very little on the ride except to tell Will her brother's address. They pulled into a nice home at the end of a quiet cul-du-sac. Great neighborhood to start a family. He banished the thought from his head. He would have to be a nomad for a little longer.

Will killed the engine. Savannah let out a loud sigh and then shifted in her seat. "Would you like to come inside? My mother is in town and I'm sure she's cooked something delicious. "

Meeting her family. No. He wasn't ready for that. "I don't want to inconvenience anyone."

"You won't be."

Will shook his head. "I think I should be going. Maybe another time."

Her expression slightly changed. In the darkness, it looked like disappointment. "Okay." She opened the car door. "Thanks again."

He watched her until the front door open and her brother appeared at the door, but he pulled out of the driveway before the door shut.

*

Savannah put on a pleasant look as she walked into the living room.

Josh stared at her. "Are you all right?"

Savannah shrugged off her coat. "Yes. Just having car trouble." *Having your windows busted out certainly qualifies as trouble.* "Do you mind giving me a ride back home?"

"Of course, but you know you can spend the night. We have an extra room."

The sound of her mother's voice cut through the conversation. "Is Savannah finally here?"

Savannah frowned and leaned close to Josh. "I'll pass on spending the night."

To his credit, Josh laughed. He never quite understood the dynamic between his mother and Savannah. Not that he would. Esther Elliott was proud of him and found fault with everything Savannah did.

"At least you can eat well tonight. Mama already cooked." He led her into the dining room.

Mama sat at the head of the table looking very much like she was holding court. A familiar look to Savannah. Mama always positioned herself to garner the maximum amount of attention and always looked the part. Tonight she wore a plum slacks suit, short boots and pearls.

Esther frowned when she spotted Savannah. "What on earth are you wearing?"

Savannah gave her a watery smile. "Hello, Mama."

Esther's eyes studied Savannah from top to bottom. "The cut of that suit is horrific. Have you gained weight?"

Savannah slouched, struggling for something to say. She knew Mama's barbs to sting, but tonight, after having her car vandalized, the hurt was magnified.

"I—"

Josh ushered Savannah to the table. "Savannah came straight from a busy day. You can question her after she eats."

Josh to the rescue again.

"Looks like she's already been doing too much of that." Esther's fake attempt to mumble ricocheted around her head. *Will said I looked nice.*

Dawn rose and briefly hugged Savannah's shoulders. "I'll get your food."

Josh sat next to Savannah. "I thought your interview on BET went really well."

"Yes, tell us about it," Dawn called from the kitchen.

Savannah smiled. "It was easier than I thought, for sure. It's generated a little buzz about the fundraiser."

Dawn stuck her head out of the kitchen, her voice thick with sorrow. "It's so sad what happened to those people." Refreshing to know someone cared.

Savannah sighed. "I see that a hundred times over in a year. It's sad that these people are so overlooked by society that only their deaths make a difference."

"Well, you're going to make sure people care, baby sis." Josh patted her hand.

Savannah exhaled, drawing in Josh's praise like a balm. "I'm going to try."

Esther folded her arms. "Well, good luck with that." Esther's words chilled, like cold water on a hot fire.

Savannah clinched her jaw. "It's not about luck. It's about caring for others." *But you wouldn't know anything about that would you?*

"I'm just saying that this is an impossible task. These people choose to come into the country illegally."

Now she sounds like Officer Grant. "And that makes it okay for them to die in the back of trucks or on freighters, all because of one bad decision?" Savannah's cheeks burned with anger. Her voice rose, along with her mother's eyebrows. "Should we just overlook the fact that these people need help?"

"Savannah." Josh's voice cut through the building tension, caution in his eyes.

Dawn hurried from the kitchen with Savannah's plate. "Here you go."

Josh seemed to breathe a sigh of relief.

Savannah quickly thanked God for her food and dug in. *If it wasn't for Mama's cooking…* Savannah took another bite of tender smothered chicken.

Esther leaned toward Josh. "Oh, I forgot to tell you that I invited someone for Easter dinner."

"Is it Dad?" Josh asked. Josh's hopefulness still amazed her. He still tried hard to have some sort of relationship with his father but his attempts failed. How can parents so dislike their children? Joshua had earned Daddy's dislike when he turned down politics for engineering but gained Mama's praise. Savannah had won the prize of Mama's displeasure, for so many reasons, but Daddy saw her as his hope to continue his legacy of public service. Strange family.

"Oh no, honey. Your daddy is far too busy. He's working on a big project he can't get away from right now." How many times had they heard that? *Too many, judging from the look on Josh's face.*

Savannah cut another piece of her chicken. "Then who is this mystery guest?"

Esther smiled wide at Savannah. "It's a surprise."

"I love surprises." Dawn clasped her hands together.

Savannah's stomach turned. Mama's surprises could be painful. Savannah's concern about the mystery guest, however, didn't linger long. She had plenty to worry about, like who had broken into her car.

The police wondered if Will was the target and not her, but after tonight, it was clear that someone was out to get her. But who? She hadn't received so much as a threat. Besides, the break-in could be random, although that pushed the bounds of logic. Why would someone go through the trouble of breaking her windows but not steal anything from the car?

Yes, Mama's mystery guest ranked way down her list of concerns.

Chapter 7

Will hated putting on a suit on the weekend. They held a bad association. Suits equaled work. Odd putting one on for church, but he wouldn't dare wear something more casual, especially not on Easter Sunday.

His mother would have said his aversion to suits resulted from his minimal church attendance. She hated the fact that he was a Mother's Day, Easter and New Year's Christian. Not that he wanted to be in that category. He longed to be free from a week of finding people hidden in trucks, locked in houses or victimized in ways that boggled the mind by a good worship service. Unfortunately, regular church attendance didn't always fit into his life. He often worked on the weekends and any other times he could attend got buried underneath exhausting days. He tried to maintain his holiday visits.

When he did go, Mom made a big deal out of it. He had to pick her up from her house and drive her to church. Today was special. Mom's church served Easter dinner each year and the women at his mother's church could burn.

He grabbed his Bible. Even with the food enticing him, he braced himself for the day. It would be hard without Jordan. Shantel would normally let him attend church with Will and Mom even if it wasn't Will's normal visitation day. Now that they...more like she decided on their new visitation arrangement, spending Sunday, or any day, with Jordan was out.

Mom waited in front of her house when he arrived. She wore a lilac suit with a huge brimmed hat, her trademark. "Good morning, baby." She climbed in and planted a kiss on his cheek. "You look nice."

Will chuckled.

She clicked her seatbelt into place. "We need to make a stop. Someone asked me for a ride to church."

As Mom gave him the directions, anxiety ballooned in Will's stomach. They were heading to the same neighborhood that Jordan lived. His anger nearly exploded when his mother instructed him to stop in front of the high rise where Shantel and Jordan lived.

"Mom—"

She held up a hand, silencing him. "I don't want to hear it, William." She opened the car door. "He called last night to see what time we were picking him up. I want to see him. If you've got a problem with that, drop us off at the church and go home."

"You're only making things worse," Will said through gritted teeth.

Mom didn't reply. She shut the door and walked up to the building, heels pounding on the sidewalk.

Will's anger raged. Why would she agree to this? Did she want to torture him? Beyond his anger, a dot of hope swelled at the thought of seeing Jordan. The month Will hadn't talked to him seemed like an eternity. Jordan probably would have a lot to fill him in on. As exciting as the day would be, it would end with the disappointment of returning Jordan back to Shantel and that joker Derrick. *Derrick, Jordan's real father.*

Mom and Jordan emerged from the building, Jordan's hand snuggly fit in his Nana's hand. He wore a little blue suit that made him look older than six and the biggest grin. Before he could contain his emotions, Will rushed from the car. He didn't think Jordan could smile any wider, but he did. The boy ran down the walkway and launched himself off the ground into Will's arms.

"Daddy," he said, his voice barely a whisper.

Will held him tight. How was he going to let this boy go?

All of Will's previous anxiety melted into happiness on the ride to the church. Jordan told Will everything about school for the past month. Including his missed project. Will fought to keep his anger in check when Jordan told him how he'd asked Shantel for help. Of course, she had too many other things to do to help him.

"I don't like Derrick," Jordan announced from the back seat.

Will peered into the rearview mirror. "You don't know him well enough."

Jordan's frown wrinkled his nose. "He's creepy. And he doesn't like to read."

"That's not a reason to not like him."

"Yes, it is. Reading is fundamental," Jordan said. "Reading builds vocabulary and improves communication skills."

Will's eyebrows rose. "That's impressive."

"Ms. Jackson says that all the time."

Will chuckled. "Well, it's impressive that you listen."

"Why can't I live with you? You like to read."

Will's heart ached. They used to curl up in their pajamas on a Saturday morning and read the newspaper.

"Jordan…" Will looked into Jordan's eyes, noting the sadness there.

"I know. Derrick is my new dad. Mom tells me all the time. Can I come see you sometime?"

Will sighed. "I'll talk to your mother." Shantel would probably fight visitations tooth and nail, unless she needed a babysitter. The least Shantel could do is let Jordan visit. After six years he should be entitled to something.

*

Easter Sunday dawned with deep plums and reds, but quickly brightened to full sunshine. Much like Savannah's emotions.

In a week's time, she'd been shot at and vandalized. She'd spent two very dark nights worrying. Officer Dunn had done her best to put Savannah at ease, but it hadn't worked. Easter morning, however, gave her the lift she needed.

As the day progressed, she felt her thoughts shift back to normal. Even Dawn mentioned that Savannah had seemed distracted for the past couple of days. She almost told them about the incident with her car, but didn't. She didn't want to sink her good mood discussing that. Even her mother, who had decided to attend church with them, couldn't combat the lightness Savannah felt.

They attended the early morning service and quickly headed back to Josh's house so that her mother could finish preparing dinner. Savannah steered clear of the kitchen, her cooking skills well below her mothers. Much to her mother's chagrin, Savannah had never learned to cook anything beyond the basics. Esther was determined to raise a proper southern lady knowledgeable in all the graces of entertaining. Savannah's marriage to Mitch should have solidified that status and her broken engagement was epic to her mother. *If she only knew...*

Mama, with Dawn's help, managed to finish all the food by 3:45. Savannah stationed herself at the front door and welcomed the dinner guests. Most of them were Josh and Dawn's friends, but Carrie joined them. As each guest arrived, Savannah's concern for her mother's mystery visitor increased. A little mystery made most gatherings interesting, but Savannah couldn't take much more drama.

At four, all the guests gathered around the table and Josh blessed the food. Savannah silently thanked God for her family, no matter how dysfunctional they could be sometimes. As everyone began to dig into the food, Esther won several compliments about her cooking. Well-earned compliments. She still didn't know how Mama managed to get her lamb so tender. Carrie remained silent, savoring each bite of food. Mama looked in Carrie's direction.

Esther beamed. "I enjoy cooking for people like you who love a good meal."

"You can cook for me anytime you like." Carrie stuffed the last piece of a homemade roll in her mouth. "I'll even pay your travel expenses."

"Mom you don't visit often enough." Josh put down his fork and glanced at Dawn. She gave him a slight nod. "I think Dawn and I have an incentive to change that."

Savannah clenched her jaw to keep her mouth shut. What was Josh doing? Didn't he realize how much easier her life was with Esther living three states away?

Josh cleared his throat. "We're having a baby."

The room erupted in cheers. Savannah sprang to her feet, squealing and ran to Dawn. Savannah hugged her fiercely and then pulled Josh into an embrace. Esther rose to embrace Dawn, also.

"I'm so happy for you," Savannah said, wiping tears from her eyes.

"I wanted to tell you, but we thought it was better to make the announcement when we found out Esther was coming."

Savannah sighed. "I'm going to be an auntie."

Dawn beamed as Josh protectively placed his hand on Dawn's stomach. They had the perfect life. Despite Savannah's joy for them, a pang of jealously hit her. She wasn't envious of them. They deserved happiness. Her own happiness proved to be a little more elusive.

Savannah stood. "That deserves a toast. Would anyone like more tea?" Several of the guests nodded.

Carrie rose, too. "I'll help."

She and Savannah gathered as many glasses as they could carry and refilled them with sweet tea. The doorbell sounded as they gathered the glasses and headed back to the dining room.

Savannah almost made it to the table.

Mitch rounded the corner from the front hallway, Esther on his arm.

Run! Savannah's mind screamed but her feet wouldn't move. Her vision narrowed and she tightened her grip on the glasses.

Esther grinned. "Everyone, this is Mitch."

Mitch's gaze skipped over all the other guests and zeroed in on Savannah. "Hi, Ladybug."

Savannah blinked a few times. Her brain struggled to absorb the shock of seeing his GQ physic standing in front of her. Curly black hair, eyes that vacillated between green and hazel and flawless skin that made most women jealous. A perfect specimen of the ethnic melting pot of his African-American mother and his Guatemalan father, possessing the best features of them both.

A very attractive monster.

"Josh and Savannah, you already know Mitch." Esther gestured toward Dawn. "This is my daughter-in-law, Dawn. I'm going to be a grandmother."

Mitch nodded toward Dawn. "Nice to meet you and congratulations."

Dawn frowned, eying her husband and Savannah. "Thank you."

Esther motioned to the table. "Savannah, why don't you sit down? I'm sure you and Mitch have lots of things to catch up on."

Before Esther could return to her seat, Josh grabbed her arm. "Mama, can I talk to you in the kitchen for a moment?"

Savannah's legs wobbled her toward the table but her mind drifted to that night in the warehouse. She shuddered.

Mitch quickly stepped toward her, taking the glasses from her hands.

She kept her head down and sat in her seat, numb and trembling. How could Mama invite Mitch to dinner?

Mitch took the seat next to her like it was assigned to him. "I guess I can't ask how you've been since I already know. Your parents have kept me updated on you and your organization."

Savannah's head swam. She fought to steady her voice for the sake of the other guests. "Yes, things are going well."

"I saw you on BET. Good stuff. The fundraiser sounds like it's going to be a big success." He inched closer to her chair.

Savannah fought to take a deep breath.

Mama and Josh returned from the kitchen and neither of them looked happy. Josh gave Savannah a sad look. Esther took her seat, back straight.

Josh returned to his seat next to Dawn. "What are you doing in town? I'm sure you're busy with running your business in Georgia." Josh's tone made it clear that he could care less about Mitch's activities.

"I'm handling some business here in the area. I'll be here for a few days. Hopefully I can catch the sights while I'm here." Mitch glanced at Savannah. "What do you say about showing me around DC?"

Mama spoke before Savannah could process Mitch's request. "She would love to."

Savannah's stomach heaved. "No."

Esther sent Savannah a narrowed eyed gaze. "Honey, you work downtown. How hard would it be to show him around? He's a guest in your city."

The room quieted.

"I can't. I don't have any time to spare." Savannah stood from the table, collecting a few plates.

Mitch followed her to just inside the kitchen door. "Ladybug."

Savannah spun to face him. "Please stop calling me that."

"Sorry. I'm just trying to talk to you." His eyes pleaded. Savannah remembered a time she would have fallen for his sad puppy look.

"I wasn't aware that we had anything to talk about."

"Look, I know things didn't end well with us."

"You were investigated by the FBI." *Among other things.*

"They didn't find anything and that was over a year ago." Mitch stepped close enough for her to smell his cologne. "I'm not going to lie. I hoped that there was still something between us." He reached out and touched her shoulder.

She pulled back.

"If not, maybe we could start over."

Savannah studied him. Why had she thought she loved him before? Was it because he was handsome, rich and powerful? The society pages thought they were a perfect couple. On the surface, they should have been. Mitch's father's sugar import business had made him a wealthy businessman. Her father's political connections put them both in the same social circles. How did she fall for him?

I didn't know who he really was.

"I think you should leave." Her voice almost sounded brave.

"I just got here and I have been looking forward to some of your mother's cooking." Mitch laughed as he left the kitchen.

Savannah sighed, closed her eyes and let her shoulders slump. She needed to pull it together before she returned to the dining room. When she opened her eyes, Mama stood in of front her with her hands on her hips and an angry glare on her face.

"Why did you send him away? I went out of my way to get him here."

"If you would have told me what you were doing, I would have told you not to waste your time."

Savannah started out of the kitchen but Esther grabbed her arm. "Listen here, young lady." Esther gave Savannah's arm a tight squeeze. "You call him and tell him you will show him around the city."

Savannah snatched her arm from Esther's grasp. "I am not a child and I will do no such thing."

Esther stepped back. "You think you aren't, but you still act like a silly little girl. Men like Mitch don't wait around for women like you."

"I never asked him to wait around for me." Savannah's voice rose to the verge of yelling.

"Watch your tone."

Savannah pushed past her and back into the dining room. Josh stood. Mitch sat in his chair like he had no intentions on leaving.

Savannah stared at her empty seat. If Mitch wouldn't leave, she would. "I've got a lot of work to do tomorrow so I'm going to head home."

"You haven't even had dessert," Dawn whined, her gaze shifting from Mitch to Esther to Savannah.

"Maybe I'll come by tomorrow if there're any leftovers." Savannah grabbed her things and was gone before anyone else could protest.

*

Jordan snoozed in the backseat, the passing streetlights illuminating his nodding head. Mom sat in silence next to Will. Jordan had played with every child in the building during the church dinner. His laughter would rise above all the other children's. A melancholy sound...that and the sound of him calling Will Daddy. For all the sadness, Will wouldn't have traded the day for anything.

"You okay?" Denise reached over and put her hand on Will's.

"Yes. Thank you for making me get him."

"I didn't make you. You did what you wanted."

"I thought it would be hard to have him around. That it would make me miss him more."

She rubbed his hand. "You will miss him terribly. I'd think you were crazy if you didn't. That doesn't mean you shouldn't spend as much time as you can with him."

Will pulled in front of the high rise. "It's going to be harder to let him go."

"Have you asked God whether or not you should transfer?"

"Mom. . . "

"I'm serious. Maybe God wants to work this out differently." She looked over her shoulder. "That little boy needs a father."

"He's got one and it's not me."

"You're the only father he knows. God commands us to take care of the fatherless. The orphans."

"He's not an orphan. He has a family. Besides, Shantel isn't going to let me be in his life. That's a part of the agreement."

"Forget the agreement. This goes deeper than that. There is no way you can convince me that God didn't put you in this boy's life only to have you leave."

"I'll pray, all right." Will didn't like the defeat he heard in his voice. Prayer was the most effective thing he could do right now. But asking God for help seemed useless. If praying brought action on God's part, there would be no crime and no broken hearts.

Will hoisted Jordan out of the back seat of the car and carried him up the walkway, his mother a few steps behind him. The doors of the high rise swished opened and building's odor hit Will in the face. He'd always hated the fact that the place smelled like it had been wallpapered with stale bread. He walked down the middle of the hall, careful not to touch the walls. They rode an even staler-smelling elevator up to the 6th floor. His mother knocked on Shantel's door. The door opened to a haggard-looking Shantel and another smell. Alcohol.

"Shantel." Will managed to keep his voice civil.

"I didn't think you were going to bring him back. Thought I was going to have to call the police." She let out a mirthless laugh. "Oh, I forgot. You are the police."

Will didn't bother explaining his job for the fifty thousandth time. Maybe she needed to think he was the police. He walked past her and tried to ignore the empty food containers, mail and clothes littered around the room.

Jordan's door stood ajar, and once Will flipped on the lamp, he saw it was immaculately clean. Jordan had taken after him in that.

No, he learned it from me.

Will lowered the boy to the bed. Jordan stirred but submitted to being undressed. Will tucked him in bed, listening to his mother's tense conversation with Shantel. Mom loved Jordan but she didn't hide the fact that Shantel wasn't her favorite person in the world. Will kissed Jordan on the forehead and flipped off the light.

"Goodnight, Daddy." Jordan's voice drifted from behind him just as he made it to the door.

"Sleep tight, buddy."

"I love you."

Will gripped the door jam. "I love you, too."

Shantel coolly appraised him when he emerged from the bedroom.

Will stepped over a pile of clothes. "Jordan told me about his project."

Shantel tensed, folding her arms. "That's not your concern anymore."

Will stepped closer. "It is when they call me. Have you taken my name off the emergency contact list?"

She flopped down on her dingy sofa. "I'll get to it."

"Do it soon. You're only making this harder for me."

"This hasn't exactly been a smooth transition for me either."

Will shook his head. Always the victim, even when she was wrong. "Derrick should be helping you with this. You two need to do what's best for Jordan."

Shantel sprang from the sofa like an alley cat ready to fight. "Don't tell me who should do what. You don't get to tell me what's best for Jordan. You're not his father."

Will sucked in a breath as if Shantel had physically hit him. "Whose fault is that?" he asked, his voice even.

"Time out." Mom stepped between them. "This is counterproductive." She turned to Shantel. "Thank you for letting Jordan spend the day with us."

Shantel pursed her lips. "Yeah, well. He would have bugged me all day if I didn't."

It took the rest of Will's self-control to keep his mouth shut as they left. In the elevator, Will punched the button for the ground floor. *How dare she make this my fault?* He jabbed the button again.

Mom gripped his shoulder. "That elevator button didn't do anything to you."

Will turned to face her. Her expression evaporated his anger. Tears ran down her cheeks. "Mom."

"I know, William. Things are going to work out. They that sow in tears shall reap in joy."

Chapter 8

Monday almost felt normal to Will. He'd spent part of the weekend with Jordan and there was work on his desk. He settled into his seat. Almost normal. Not that he expected to accomplish much with his case. Then again, that was normal, too. Sometimes a case just stalled, but that didn't mean that Will would stop ferretting out leads.

He had a normal to-do list, too. He needed to call his mother, first to thank her again for arranging the day with Jordan and then to check if she needed any help with dinner with Savannah tomorrow. Which brought him to the next item on his list: calling Savannah. Had she recovered from Friday night? Will wasn't naïve to think that a few days would ease her pain, but it may be better than the teary-eyed state he'd left her in on Friday.

He picked up his desk phone and dialed Savannah's office number from memory. Her perky receptionist answered and in two clicks transferred Will to Savannah's desk.

"Good morning, Agent Anderson...I mean, Will."

He smiled and tucked the receiver between his shoulder and cheek. "Good morning. Are you doing better?"

"I am." She sighed. "Officer Dunn called this morning. They didn't find much to go on."

"The garage has security cameras."

"Unfortunately, the perpetrators knew where they were and kept their faces hidden."

Will fumbled with a pen with his free hand. That means someone put some planning into this. Not that he wanted to be the target of the shooting, but he would feel better if he was. Savannah was vulnerable. "As much as I hate to say this, you may want to seriously think about your enemies. Are you sure you don't know anyone who would want to intimidate or hurt you?"

Savannah remained quiet for so long that Will thought the phone had possibly disconnected. "Savannah?"

"Oh, sorry. I can't think of anyone who would want to hurt me."

Your silence suggests you do. "If you have any thoughts, no matter how small, you should tell Officer Dunn. I've solved many cases on solely a gut feeling someone had."

Her voice rang tense. "I promise I will tell Officer Dunn of anything that comes to mind."

"Okay." *She's obviously not ready to talk about this.* Will switched gears. "Are you looking forward to dinner with my mother?"

"I can't wait. I'm so excited."

"Great. Don't forget. Six thirty."

"Right." He heard her inhale. "Thanks for calling, Will. It's good to know you care—you're watching out for me."

I do care about you. He bit back the words. He wasn't…no shouldn't, admit that right now. "See you Tuesday."

Will returned the phone to the base and felt chilled. Savannah's voice had warmed his ear. Logic screamed for caution, but his heart thrummed in his chest.

*

The interview with BET, although a good thing, brought more work to Plateau. Savannah had worked straight through the rest of the day Monday and all of Tuesday, but Will was never far from her thoughts. Her excitement about dinner with Will and Denise hiked into giddy levels around four o'clock. Each time she thought of spending the evening with them, she couldn't contain her smile. She would rebuke herself, only to find the same sappy grin on her face five minutes later.

Carrie came in with her normal end of the day visit, handing off the remainder of the messages and getting her marching orders for the next morning.

"What's up with you?" she asked as she laid a folder on Savannah's desk.

"What do you mean?"

Carrie put her hand on her hip. "You've been smiling all day."

Savannah tried to look stern. "That's unusual?"

"For you, yes."

Savannah placed the folder in her inbox. "Are you saying I walk around looking glum most of the time?"

Carrie let out a nervous laugh. "Not to sound negative, but yes. You've never smiled this much since I've started working for you."

Carrie was right. She hadn't had much to be happy about in the past year.

"I'll try and smile more." She flashed Carrie a huge cheesy grin.

"It looks good on you. Good night."

Savannah quickly shut down her office, remembering Will's words about dinner starting on time. Much like in the Elliott household. She wanted to give herself enough extra time in case traffic was bad.

Just as she turned off the last of the office lights, her cell phone rang.

She let out a loud sigh when she read the number on her cell phone's LCD readout.

Mama.

After Sunday's dinner, she secretly hoped her mother would have excommunicated Savannah from the family. Dawn had given her a play-by-play of what happened after Savannah left. Mitch didn't leave, chatting with the other guests like he belonged. Dawn told her that her mother had apologized profusely for Savannah behavior, probably motivated by Mama's embarrassment.

Savannah looked at her phone as it gave off its second ring. *Ignore it.* No, that was rude. Don't be rude. That was the golden rule her family lived by.

No matter how much you don't want to go to your father's functions and meet people who only care about you because they want to get in good with your father. No matter how many reporters slander your name and make up lies about you, don't be rude.

She answered the phone on the third ring.

"I didn't think you were going to pick up."

I wasn't. "What can I do for you, Mama?"

"So formal. You could be a little nicer after that stunt you pulled Sunday. Mitch was very disappointed at not being able to talk to you very long."

"I've had a very long day. Is there something specific you wanted?"

Mama huffed. "I wanted to see if you had eaten dinner."

"Is this another ambush?"

"Why would you say that?" Her mother's voice gave a little squeak.

"Mama?"

"Mitch just wants to talk to you. I think he's still in love with you."

Savannah fought off the wave of nausea. "I'm sorry for him, but I'm not interested."

"Savannah, dear, you're not getting any younger. You need to start thinking about doing something meaningful like starting a family."

Savannah seethed. "I'm helping people through the worse time of their lives. This is meaningful."

"I don't want to argue about this anymore. Mitch is on his way to pick you up."

Savannah glanced up at her office door as if Mitch would be standing there, and then shook her head. Carrie would have locked the doors when she left. He couldn't get in unless he was a ghost. "Mama, you didn't."

"Someone has to do it. You won't."

"Good bye." Savannah ended the call, quickly grabbed her things, and bolted down the hallway. She would be long gone by the time Mitch arrived. She wished for a backdoor, but that was one of the problems with renting a space in an office building. One way in and one way out. The front door in view, she increased her pace, jostling her coat, purse and briefcase.

A rapping on the glass doors caught her attention. Mitch stood at the door, one hand in his pocket. She skidded to a stop.

One way in and one way out.

She tried to steady her trembling hands as she turned the locks on the door and opened it.

Mitch wore a knowing smile. "Looks like I arrived just in time."

"I was just telling Mama on the phone that I've had a long day." *I should have known Mitch was already here. Mama wouldn't leave that to chance.*

"Great. Let's grab some dinner. Surely you were going to eat something."

Savannah stayed just inside the doorway. As if the threshold was some kind of protection. "Actually, I have plans for the evening."

Mitch stepped closer. "Really? You mother said you were free."

"My mother doesn't manage my schedule." She willed herself not to slam and lock the door.

He gave her a sad, almost convincing look. "Savannah, I only want to talk about whatever went wrong between us." He took another step toward her. "I don't believe it was just the FBI investigation. You moved away even after the investigation didn't turn up anything."

He reached across the threshold and caressed her face.

She flinched.

The air around her seemed to drop twenty degrees as he stroked her cheek and then laced his fingers through her hair. "You used to enjoy this."

She shuddered and turned her head away from his hand. "We don't have anything to talk about."

"I think we do. I can wait longer. I gave you your space here in DC. I left you alone but we will have to talk eventually." He leaned against the door as if he would wait there until her tongue loosened. "It might surprise you what I already know."

Savannah's gaze snapped up to his. His face looked calm, but there was something else there. A look of recognition. *Could he know? How could he know?*

"I'll be around. Call me when you're ready to talk."

"Good night, Mitch." Savannah stepped back and began to close the door.

Mitch stopped it with his hand. "Thought you were leaving." Mitch's smile iced her veins.

"I--I just remembered something I have to finish."

Mitch nodded and departed. Savannah closed the door and quickly turned all the locks. So much for smiling more.

*

Will removed his coat, hung it in his mother's closet and took a deep breath. The air permeated with the smell of fried chicken. He rolled up his sleeves and dropped his cufflinks into his pocket. He'd left the office early to help mom, but from the smell of things, the food was probably done. That was a good thing. It would help establish that Savannah was mom's guest and not his. He didn't want her to feel like he was pursuing her…as much as he would like to, he couldn't.

He joined mom in the kitchen. She stood at the stove, back to him. "Hey, Mom." He leaned around her and planted a peck on her cheek.

She smiled. "Hey, baby."

His suspicions about the food were right. Everything seemed ready. The paper towel-lined bowl of fried chicken sat just in front of him. He lifted a wing, but then grunted and dropped it on the counter. It would have helped if he'd stolen a cooler piece.

"That's what you get." Mom's focus never left the remaining pieces in the hot grease. "Go ahead and put that one to the side. That's your piece."

Will blew on his fingertips. "I can't believe you can still do that."

"What? Knowing when you're stealing chicken? A mother knows her child. Besides, you've been stealing chicken since you were tall enough to reach the counter." She lifted the last pieces out of the hot grease. "It wasn't hard to figure out who it was since you were the only other person around."

Will grinned. "I thought you didn't know it was me."

She let out a short laugh and shook her head. "Did you tell Savannah that dinner starts at six thirty?"

Will glanced at the clock on the stove. Six-twenty. Maybe Savannah changed her mind. "Yes. I'm sure she's on her way."

"Help me move this food to the table."

Mom had gone all out. Cabbage, mashed sweet potatoes, chicken, and dinner rolls. Mom had been so happy to learn that Savannah was from the south, even though Will didn't know exactly what part of Georgia she was from. He would find out tonight…in a casual, non-dating way.

As they arranged the last of the dishes, the doorbell rang.

Mom disappeared into the kitchen. "Can you get that for me?"

So much for making it seem like Savannah was mom's guest.

He opened the door and the sight of Savannah took his breath away. She wore a pale green coat and clutched flowers in her hand. The beauty of the flowers didn't compare to the bright smile on her face.

"Am I late?" Her words rushed out in a huff.

The glow of the sunlight caught the tips of her hair and his heart tripped. "No, you're right on time."

She stepped inside and inhaled. "Something smells wonderful."

He helped her out of her coat. The soft tips of her hair brushed his knuckles as he did, further unnerving him. The black dress she wore stopped just below her knee and modestly hugged her curves. He swallowed hard.

Mom came from the kitchen. "Savannah. Welcome." She leaned back and gave Savannah a once over. "Aren't you a cutie?"

The blush on Savannah's cheeks made her even cuter. "These are for you." She held the flowers out to Mom.

"Give me a hug first." Mom embraced her tightly and Savannah let out a squeaky laugh. "Someone in your line of work deserves all the hugs they can get."

Maybe he should give Savannah a hug, too. *Stop it.*

Mom put the flowers in a vase and sat them in the middle of the table. Will pulled out Mom and Savannah's seat, purposely steering Mom between he and Savannah. When he sat, he realized his plan backfired. He and Savannah were face-to-face.

"Honey, I hope you don't mind me blessing the food. I give thanks to God no matter the guest."

Savannah grinned. "No, please do."

Mom prayed a short prayer and they started passing bowls around the table.

"Everything looks so incredible." Savannah ladled cabbage on her plate.

"When Will told me you were from the south, I figured you'd appreciate some soul food since you're so far from home."

Savannah looked up at Will, a smile on her lips. "That was very thoughtful of him."

The bowl of potatoes slipped in his fingers. He caught it before it hit the table.

Mom began questioning Savannah like a FBI agent. Savannah was from Atlanta. Her brother lived in Upper Marlboro. She had relocated to DC one year ago and opened her non-profit.

"Dealing with human trafficking is taxing on the soul," Mom said. "I remember when Will got assigned to the Civil Rights squad."

Will shook his head. "Taxing isn't the word for it."

Savannah adjusted her napkin in her lap. "I thought I'd seen tragedy when I helped with my father's AIDS awareness campaign, but that paled in comparison to what I've seen in the past months. Sometimes it still boggles the mind."

Will nodded. "I can't understand how people can just stand by and do nothing when they know something is wrong. That upsets me just as much as the criminals who perpetrate the crimes."

Savannah coughed and her entire face turned red. Will sprang from the table and rushed to her side.

"Oh, my," Denise said and proceeded to clap Savannah hard on the back. Savannah's eyes watered.

Will leaned close. "Say something."

"I--" Savannah said, but the rest of her words were swallowed up in another fit of coughing.

"She can still talk. She'll be fine, Mom," Will said. Mom promptly stopped pounding her back.

After a few seconds of silence, Savannah gave a weak smile. "I'm good," she said her voice raspy. Since he'd knelt next to her and put his arm around the back of her chair, they were right at eye level.

"Thank you," she murmured.

Too close. Will scurried back to his side of the table.

Once Savannah composed herself and took a few swallows of water, she turned to Will's mother. "I attended one of your forums when I first moved to DC."

Mom's eyebrows shot up. "Really?"

Savannah nodded. "Georgetown University. You were speaking on the changing face of racism."

Will remembered that forum. He'd stood in the back beaming with pride listening to his mother speak. Savannah must have been on the other side of the room because he would have remembered her face.

"You hinted about how you got into civil rights. I was wondering if I could hear the whole story."

Mom took a deep breath. Over thirty years later and Will had never seen her tell this story without a struggle.

Will spoke for her. "My father was a civil rights activist, too. Shortly after I was born, he, mom and I took a trip to Mississippi for a protest rally. Even in the seventies, some places in the south still hadn't embraced desegregation."

Mom gripped her napkin. "My husband was arrested at the rally and it took me almost twenty-four hours to get the bail money. When I showed up at the jail, Bryce was dead." Mom shook her head. "No one knew what happened to him. Nobody saw anything. I kept asking and asking, but I couldn't find out anything about how he died."

The room grew quiet. No matter how many times he'd heard the story of his father's demise, Will's heart still ached. Despite the fact that he had no memories of his dad, it didn't ease the grief. He grew up without a father. He didn't realize how much that had impacted him until Jordan came along. He vowed his son would not grow up without him.

Mom's voice grew thick with emotion. "All I wanted to know was what happened. The more I pestered them, the more famous I became. After a while, I realized that in his death, Bryce had given me the perfect platform to promote the message he'd fought so hard to get out."

Tears welled in Savannah's eyes. "Wow," she whispered.

Mom reached over and patted Will's hand. "I couldn't be prouder that my son followed in his father's footsteps, although in a very different way."

Will shrugged. "I figured if there was one honest cop in the jail, my dad wouldn't have died. I wanted to make sure no one else ever lost their dad because honest people wouldn't stand up."

Savannah dabbed her eyes with her napkin. "That's funny how you and your husband used to get arrested and your son goes into law enforcement."

Will glanced at his mom and she laughed. "That's the family joke."

"It wasn't a joke when the FBI did my background check," Will said with a chuckle.

Mom glanced at the table "Wow. That was a heavy topic for a dinner. There's still a lot of food left over."

Will patted his stomach. "I'm stuffed."

Savannah grinned. "Me, too."

Mom rose from the table. "I think I'll run some of this over to my neighbor. She's elderly and doesn't get out much. You kids mind?"

Savannah waved her hand. "Not at all. We can start the dishes."

"Nonsense. Will can start the dishes. You're a guest."

Will collected the plates, carried them to the kitchen and groaned. Not from having to do the dishes but from being alone with Savannah. He hadn't planned on that.

*

Once Denise left, Savannah slipped out of her chair and followed Will to the kitchen.

Will ran water in the sink. "Sorry about the dinner topic. Kinda depressing."

"You guys are inspiring."

Will laughed. "I would have rather talked about something else."

"Like what?"

He looked over his shoulder at her as she scraped the plates in the trash. "You. What it was like being a governor's daughter."

Savannah smirked. "That is an equally depressing subject."

"Okay. Next subject. Do you have a boyfriend?"

"Still depressing." She prayed he wouldn't ask her the last time she had one.

Will chuckled. "Is there anything good about your life?"

"I'm going to be an auntie. My sister-in-law is expecting. She told us Easter Sunday." Her mind flashed back to Sunday dinner and Mitch's appearance.

"Congratulations. You don't look overjoyed."

"I am. Sadly, that's the only happy thing that came out that dinner."

"Yeah, I had a bittersweet Easter, too." He plunked in the first of the dishes. "So what else happened that made dinner unhappy?"

Savannah hesitated. How would Will react to hearing about Mitch.

He raised an eyebrow. "You know about my family's history. Dish."

Savannah leaned her hip against one of the counters. He had shared some pretty heavy stuff. It wouldn't hurt to tell him some of her history with Mitch, but not all of it. "I don't have a boyfriend, but I do have an ex-fiancée, Mitch Alverez, that wants me back."

Will scowled. "You want me to investigate him for you?"

She let out a snort and then laughed at the deadpan serious look on Will's face. *He would do it if I asked.* "No, he's already been investigated by the FBI."

"Really?"

"It gets better. My mother invited him to Easter dinner without telling me."

Will grimaced. "Oh, man."

"I come from the kitchen with a glass of sweet tea and there he was. My mother is convinced that I've passed up the perfect man."

Will paused, glancing over his shoulder. "Was he?"

Savannah's stomach fluttered when they made eye contact. Was he just asking for conversation sake? "No, but Mama will not let it go."

"Would it help if you told her you were involved with someone?"

What if I were involved with you? Savannah stared at Will's back, watching his muscles flex under his shirt as he washed the dishes. She resisted the urge to slip her arms around his waist and press her face between his shoulder blades. "She would know I was lying. I've been too busy to date."

"If you were involved with someone, it wouldn't be a lie."

Will's matter of fact tone made her smile. "No, it wouldn't."

*

Will chastised himself for his line of questioning. Yes, he'd found out what he wanted to know, that Savannah was single, but the information was useless. He was not in a position to take advantage of it.

Despite his mother's instruction, Savannah soon fell in beside him and helped him with the dishes. She dried and stored each item with care. Will fought to keep his mind on his task with the scent of Savannah's perfume and her presence swirling around the small space. Occasionally, their arms would brush and Will half-expected a spark to pop. He had to get out of this kitchen before something did ignite.

Thirty minutes later, the kitchen was clean. They'd even packed up all the leftover food, but Mom still hadn't returned. Will suspected that his mother's delay was deliberate.

Will walked to the sofa and Savannah followed. "I don't know what's keeping my mother so long. Would you like a cup of coffee?"

Savannah shook her head. "Not if I plan to sleep tonight."

She took the seat next to him, her knee brushing his, and his heart pounded. When was the last time he reacted like this to a woman? Not since Shantel. To think he thought he was in love all those years ago. Shantel couldn't compare to the type of woman Savannah appeared to be.

"Do you think your mother is all right?" Savannah's question brought him back to the present.

He grinned. "She's fine. I suspect my mother and your mother have something in common."

"What's that?"

"Their unwanted matchmaking attempts."

Will's heart warmed when Savannah laughed. "I guess they figure we need some help. I only wished my mother realized how busy I am running Plateau."

"I know what you mean."

Savannah stifled a yawn. "As enjoyable as this evening is, I think I should head home."

Mom would be disappointed. A strange sense of his own disappointment slowly ballooned in his chest as he walked to the closet and Savannah followed. No, he did not encourage his mother's matchmaking stunt, but it was nice to be alone with Savannah. Even if they were just washing the dishes.

"Let me get your coat."

He held her coat as she slid her arms in her sleeves. He took his time opening the door and walking her down the block to her car. The chill of the April evening immediately seeped through his shirt.

Savannah walked to a little black car, obviously a rental.

"You haven't got your car back?"

Savannah stuffed her hands in her pockets. "Not yet. Officer Dunn said it wouldn't be too much longer."

That's unusual. "Did she say why?"

"She said they wanted to check a few more things. I wish. . . " she started. "I had a wonderful evening. I don't want to talk about that." He couldn't make out all the details of her face, but her eyes briefly caught the glow from the streetlights. If this were more than a dinner to meet his mother, he would have tried to make more out of this little walk than it was. Maybe even hold her hand.

She fished her keys from her purse. "Please thank your mother for the wonderful dinner."

Will nodded. "I know she enjoyed your company."

Savannah smiled. "Well, goodnight." She reached over and pulled him into a short hug. This time he didn't waste time returning the embrace. She felt warm in his arms. Yeah, like he needed any more memories of Savannah in his head tonight when he went to bed.

He watched her drive down the street. *If only. . .* that was a loaded wish. If only Jordan was his son. If only he wasn't transferring to California. He turned and headed back to the house, shifting his thoughts. No sense dwelling on it.

Chapter 9

How many days would it take to get Savannah out of his mind? She'd occupied his thoughts all night and a new day didn't seem to have the power to dethrone her. Work was his best shot for reining in his musings, but he'd caught himself daydreaming three times in the first hour and a half at his desk.

His mother hadn't help. When she had returned from her extra long visit with her neighbor, she had nothing but good things to say about Savannah. Mom had practically made wedding plans despite Will's reminders that he was transferring. Mom even managed to use her like of Savannah to strengthen her position. Savannah was another reason why Will shouldn't transfer. If it weren't for his situation with Jordan, he would be reconsidering his move for Savannah's sake.

Will once again pushed his thoughts of Savannah to the back of his mind, knowing she wouldn't stay there long, and focused on the few leads he had on his case. The sketch was the best shot of moving forward.

He dialed Officer Grant for an update but got voicemail instead. He left a short message and hung up. He looked at the ledger again. That was the longest shot, but right now, it was all he had. He slid the book to him and opened it.

His cell phone, set on vibrate, rumbled across the desk. An unfamiliar number popped up on the screen.

"Mr. Anderson." He recognized Ms. Jackson's voice. "I know you asked me to call Jordan's mother, but she's not answering her phone."

Will's gaze drifted to Jordan's picture. "I spoke to her about the project and—"

"I'm sorry Mr. Anderson, but this is not about the project."

Will slowed, his mind shifted back to a call he'd gotten from Ms. Jackson two months ago. That phone call had sent him speeding to the hospital. Jordan had hurt himself on the playground. It had also started a chain of events that ruined his life. "Is Jordan all right?"

She laughed. "I'm sorry. He's fine. The power is out here and we are dismissing early. Aftercare has to close down, too. I called Jordan's mother…" Her trailing words informed Will of what he already knew. Shantel hadn't answered her phone.

Will glanced at his watch. It read 2:45pm. "I can be there in fifteen minutes."

"Thank you, Mr. Anderson."

Will trotted down to Agent Carter's office. His boss looked up when he knocked on the doorframe. "Is everything all right?"

"The power is out at my son's-" *he's not my son,* "-at Jordan's school and they can't get a hold of his mother."

"Go. See you tomorrow."

"Thanks."

*

Savannah's uncertainty increased with every step she took toward the FBI substation where Will worked. She didn't have to come and see him to thank him for inviting her to dinner at his mother's house. She could have called, thus her discomfort. Even after spending a wonderful evening together, she still wanted to see him in person.

The morning had floated by on memories of her dinner with Will and Denise. Never before had she connected with two people like she had with them. They understood the struggles of human rights work and despite the heartbreak they witnessed, were committed to improving the lives of those in need. She'd enjoyed the fact that Denise educated others about the importance of civil rights, Will's work in catching criminals and her efforts to help the victims created a mosaic of different ways to approach the same problem.

She wanted to believe that that camaraderie was the only reason for the contentment she felt, but that wouldn't be the whole truth.

Will had played a huge role. He was everything Mitch wasn't: Kind, compassionate, professional and brave. How had she ever believed she was in love with Mitch? Even before she knew about his dark side?

The sun seemed to shine a path to the FBI substation. Her stomach twisted at the thought of how Will might react to her showing up again unannounced. He seemed not to mind the last visit, but another one might be too much. Mama would be mortified if she knew Savannah was being this forward with a man. Of course, Mama's idea of being *forward* was a little extreme. This wasn't being forward. It was just a little encouragement. Not horrible since she suspected that Will wasn't exactly indifferent to her.

She opened the lobby door and stepped inside, but nearly stopped. Will strode across the lobby with purpose, shoving his arms in his coat. He spotted her, his gait slowed until he stood in front of her.

She gave him a nervous smile. "Hi, Will."

He didn't exactly smile, but it wasn't a frown either. More like confusion. "Hi. What are you doing here?"

Savannah fought back a flinch. Maybe she had read him wrong. "I-I thought I would stop by to thank you for dinner. I had a great time."

Her heart lifted when he smiled. "You're welcome. I had a good time, too."

"Are you on your way out?" *Stupid question, Savannah.* Will made her nervous, the good kind of nervous.

"Yes, I have to pick up . . . " He shifted uncomfortably. "I have an errand to run."

131

She stepped back. "Oh. Okay."

Still facing her, Will stepped around her, and then stopped. "Maybe I'll call you tonight."

She grinned. "Okay."

He took another reluctant step away from her. "Sorry about you coming all the way over here and I'm on my way out."

Savannah waved her hand. "This isn't too far from my office."

"Right." He glanced at his watch. "I'm sorry but I really must go."

She laughed and made a shooing motion. "Talk to you later."

He grinned and trotted out the door. She walked back to her car relieved. Will's hesitation to leave suggested he wanted to stay with her. She would, however, call first next time.

*

Will forced himself to drive the speed limit to Jordan's school in Southeast DC. Traffic added fuel to his anger. Shantel being MIA didn't help. When would she get it through her stubborn skull that she needed to answer her phone? What if Will hadn't been available? He suspected that Shantel banked on Will being available.

Cars crowded the street and very angry-looking crossing guards directed traffic near the front door of the school. Will eased his car forward. His fight with guilt progressed equally as slow. Savannah had come to see him. His heart hammered when he saw her standing in the lobby. He couldn't forget her look of disappointment when he said he was going to run an errand.

An errand. Like Jordan was a loaf of bread or a gallon of milk. He couldn't bring himself to tell her about Jordan. He feared her reaction. Silly since there wasn't anything going on between them anyway. Not that he could have explained his situation with Jordan in the few seconds they'd talked in the lobby.

He parked his car a block away. The main hall of the school bustled with activity and the sunlight provided just enough light for Will to make out the faces of the children flowing through the hall.

He navigated to Ms. Jackson's classroom.

"Jordan, your dad is here." One of the other children yelled.

Ms. Jackson looked up from her desk. "Bus riders, please line up at the door," she called out and then turned to Will. "Thanks for coming so quickly."

"No problem."

Jordan ran to Will's side, wedging his body next to Will.

"I didn't get a chance to distribute homework, so he'll probably have double tomorrow."

Jordan groaned and Will laughed. "Thanks, Ms. Jackson."

Before they could make it out of the building, Jordan had speed-talked his way through a half of day of events.

Will rubbed his head. "You hungry, buddy?"

"Can we get pizza?" Jordan gave Will his best puppy dog look.

Will stifled a smile. "Hmmm, I don't know."

"Please?" Jordan drew out the word. He flashed Will a huge grin.

I would give you the moon if I could.

*

Savannah entered Plateau to find Officer Dunn sitting on one of the couches and her heart sank. Officer Dunn's communications normally meant bad news.

Savannah put on a smile to cover her discomfort. "This must be the day for surprise visits. I just went to see Agent Anderson."

Officer Dunn gave Savannah a knowing smile. "How was he?"

"Well, but on his way out. We didn't visit long." Savannah's face flushed. Why did she feel the need to explain herself to Officer Dunn?

"Good to know. I was planning to contact him today." She looked around the lobby. "Do you have a few moments?"

"Let's go to my office."

Officer Dunn studied everything as they walked to Savannah's office. Savannah motioned to a seat.

Officer Dunn studied the office, particularly the windows, before she sat. "I have some new developments concerning your car."

Savannah leaned back in her chair, trying to brace herself and temper her rising alarm. "That's a good thing, though, right?"

Officer Dunn's serious expression didn't change. "Ms. Elliott, your windows were shot out."

Savannah exhaled with a tremble. "They looked like they were busted with a crowbar or something."

"That's what we thought at first. The security footage showed them shooting out the windows. We recovered bullets embedded in your car. That's why we had to keep it little longer."

Savannah clasped her hands to her chest. "How did they manage to fire the shots without being heard."

Dunn frowned. "Used a silencer, which has me worried. That's a little high tech for our normal local criminal."

What if I had been in that car? I would have been dead and no one would have heard the shots. "Have you—"

"Sent the bullets off for ballistic analysis? Yes." She tilted her head. "I'm actually quite concerned for you, Ms. Elliott. Are you sure you don't know of anyone who would want to hurt you?"

Savannah shook her head, but when she did, Mitch's face surfaced like a vapor. Mitch didn't want to hurt her. "I can't think of anyone."

"Maybe someone who wants to hurt your father."

Savannah attention snapped to Dunn. "Why would you ask that?"

Officer Dunn held up her hands. "Because I have to. You have to admit someone shooting out your windows is a little strange. Especially for someone who doesn't really have any enemies."

"So you think someone might be targeting me to get to my father?"

"Not for certain, but I have to explore the possibility."

Officer Dunn finished up the visit by telling Savannah that MPD would be paying close attention to her case. It was supposed to be reassuring, but it left Savannah's stomach twisted in knots anyway.

*

Will picked up Jordan's favorite pizza on the way home. As soon as they got in the house, Will changed from his suit into some comfortable sweats. Even though having Jordan was an unexpected development and Jordan normally didn't visit on weeknights, it felt more like their normal routine. His anger at Shantel had abated a little. Hard to stay angry when the by-product of Shantel's irresponsibility was watching Jordan climb the stairs to his room.

Jordan raced in a small space at the foot of the bed. "My room! My room!" he yelled. Then he collapsed on the end of his bed, arms stretched above his head.

Will leaned against the doorframe. "Pizza's going to get cold."

Jordan didn't open his eyes. "Just let me enjoy the moment."

Will guffawed. "Ok, I'll see you downstairs. See if you've got something to change into in there."

Jordan appeared five minutes later dressed in a t-shirt, a pair of shorts and white socks. He climbed up into the chair next to Will, smiling.

"I'll bless the food." Jordan volunteered. Will bowed his head and listen to Jordan thank God for the food, Ms. Jackson and the best dad in the world. A lump formed in Will's throat. Why did the good guys have such problems? Shantel didn't care about this little boy enough to answer her phone, but he had to live through having his heart ripped out, loving this boy more than life.

As soon as he'd prayed the last word, Jordan took a big bite of his slice of pizza. Then he promptly launched into an update of his life since the last time he'd seen Will. For a six year old, Jordan had amassed an impressive vocabulary. Talking to him was engaging.

"So Dad, what do you know about girls?"

Will choked on his apple juice. Was it time to have that talk already? "A lot."

Jordan gazed intently at Will.

"Maybe I should ask you what you know about girls." Will lifted another piece of pizza out of the box.

"They're confusing."

Will laughed. "Ain't that the truth."

"Gabby keeps showing me her shoes." Jordan frowned and shook his head. "Every day, she asks me if I like them. They are nice shoes."

"Do you tell her you like them?"

"Yeah. But she asks every day." Jordan raised his hands, confusion on his face. "The other day, she told me I was hot and asked for my number."

Will frowned. "She asked for your number?"

"Yeah, Dad. She gave me hers."

"What?"

Jordan jumped up from the table and ran to his room. "I'll show you," he called as he ran up the stairs. Two minutes later he returned with a piece a paper. Panting, he handed it to Will. Will slowly unfolded the paper. Gabby had scrawled her number in crayon. Jordan stood, face serious, as Will read the paper. Will forced back a grin. At least getting a girl's number in crayon was original.

Jordan sighed. "I didn't want her number. I like playing with her but I don't want to call her."

Will smiled. Six year-old boys still thought girls were gross. "Then don't call her."

Jordan flopped down in his chair. "I think this is sexual harassment. Can you come and talk to her?"

"What do you know about sexual harassment?"

"I watch TV, Dad."

"Too much I see."

"What else am I supposed to do while Mom is gone?"

Will sat his slice of pizza on his plate. "Gone?"

"Yeah. Sometimes she runs errands and I have to stay home."

"By yourself?"

"Well, the Chung family is home. If I get lonely, I go over and watch TV with them. Mom probably had an errand to run tonight and that's why she didn't pick me up."

Will clenched his jaw. His mind flooded with things to say about Shantel, but none were appropriate to say out loud. As much as he didn't like Shantel's behavior, he wouldn't badmouth her in front of Jordan. Besides, Jordan would probably understand exactly what he was saying.

"I'll call her again."

"She won't answer. She turns her phone off when she runs errands. Can we watch TV?"

Jordan didn't wait for an answer before he bounded over and picked up the TV remote. Fuming, Will cleared the table. He shouldn't be surprised. Shantel had showed questionable parenting skills from the beginning. She had informed him about the pregnancy like she was talking about a pimple.

She had come to the apartment he used to have in Baltimore. He'd rented the place his first year out of the police academy. His life had fallen into a routine. He'd been assigned as a beat cop. Most people dreaded the job, but in his head he'd imagined himself as Officer Friendly. He'd even visited a few schools and talked to kids. He loved to see their little faces staring up at him like he could conquer the world. Soon, he would have a child of his own. The idea thrilled him, but he quickly suppressed it. Was he ready to be a father?

Just as the joy of possibility being a father crept into his mind, the challenges of being a father soon followed. Would he be able to provide for the child with just his police salary? What about he and Shantel? Should he marry her? No, he didn't want to marry her. They'd only been dating for four months and her pregnancy was a result of one careless moment. He'd regretted it the next morning. He should have taken it as a sign.

Her announcement of pregnancy had stunned him. More surprising was the fact that she'd already set up an appointment for an abortion. Will remembered her expression when he told her he actually wanted to keep the baby.

She had folded her arms and glared at him. "I figured you wouldn't want it."

"Can I think about it?" he'd asked her, placing his hand on top of hers.

"What is there to think about?" Shantel had snapped, pulling her hand away. "This was a mistake and it shouldn't ruin our relationship. We weren't thinking. I'll even pay half of the cost."

Will stood from where he'd been sitting on the couch and turned to face her. "I'm not looking for a discount. I'm not comfortable with killing a helpless baby."

He remembered how her pretty face contorted. Shantel was very pretty. There was, however, always this ugliness hovering just below the surface of her flawless skin and with the right prompting, it would surface.

"It's not a baby yet."

"It is. It's my baby."

Shantel had gone through the pregnancy like she faced a death sentence. Will had to call her and remind her about her prenatal appointments, and often accompany her. Although her whining and complaining increased with each month, Will's love for the little person growing in her womb increased. He'd nearly cried as he watched Jordan's heartbeat on the ultrasound but Shantel's attitude made him restrain his tears.

"Dad, come on. American Idol is on!" Jordan yelled from the living room, jolting Will back to the present, a present where Jordan was here with him. Will placed their glasses in the sink. He'd done all that fighting to keep him only now to have Jordan taken away from him.

Chapter 10

Will's phone buzzed, bringing him fully awake in seconds. He fumbled for it, picked it up, and read the new text message. It was Jordan's school's automated notification system. They had restored the power. Time to get moving. He swung his legs out of bed.

"Jordan."

Will walked down the hall. Jordan's room was silent. *Guess he's still not a morning person.* Will hadn't forgotten that it took Jordan a while to get any traction in the morning.

He knocked on the doorframe and Jordan rolled over. "Time for school."

Jordan lay there for a moment, and then grinned. "Okay, Dad."

To Will's surprise, the boy got out of bed and immediately started getting ready. Will went down to the laundry room to retrieve Jordan's uniform from the dryer. He had washed the night before and stayed up to put it in the dryer while he waited for Shantel to call. He took it up to Jordan and came back down to start breakfast. As nice as it was having Jordan there, he would have to brace himself for when Jordan went back to Shantel.

Joy and melancholy battled in him. His emotions had become a confusing mix the past couple of days. Not only did he have to battle with Jordan, he had to battle his emotions with leaving his mother and now, his feelings for Savannah. He'd promised to try and call her last night, but had gotten involved with Jordan. It would have been nice to hear her voice. It would have also been a hard conversation, wanting to open his heart to her but not being able to. He would have to guard his heart on multiple fronts until his transfer.

Jordan talked through breakfast and the car ride to the school. Will parked down the block and they walked the rest of the way hand in hand…and Jordan kept on talking. Will listened, his dread growing. Once he dropped Jordan off, he would go back to Shantel and away from him. *This is for the best, remember?* When Shantel first confessed the truth of Jordan's parentage to Will, he'd agreed with Shantel that Jordan didn't need to be confused. Now he wasn't so sure. Jordan seemed to understand more than Will or Shantel gave him credit for.

They reached the door in the throng of other children entering.

Jordan stopped and looked up at Will. "Are you coming to pick me up this afternoon?"

All the fortification he'd built up preparing for this moment vanished. His heart sank. "Probably not. Yesterday was special."

Jordan glanced down at his shoes, his shoulders drooping. "I wish every day could be special."

Will squatted in front of the boy. "You know if you ever need anything, I'll be here." *Don't make promises you can't keep,* logic warned. But he'd do everything in his power to keep this one.

Jordan grinned and hugged Will. "I know, Dad."

Will watched the boy trot up the stairs and started an intense conversation with another little boy. *If only…*

Will turned and headed back to his car, his thoughts stormy even though the sun shone brightly. Best and worse way to start a day.

His phone buzzed. He answered, hoping it was Savannah. He grimaced when he heard Officer Grant's voice.

"Good morning, Agent Anderson. I thought you'd want to know that I got the sketch back from Rawls."

"Good." *That would give him something to do when he got back to the office.* "Can you send over a copy?"

"Already on its way."

"Thanks."

He almost sighed aloud, relief coming from the idea of having something to do when he got back in the office. He would have to put out a BOLO for the man in the sketch. He would also have to arrange to talk to Marisol again…which meant he had a legitimate reason to call Savannah today. He would get to spend more time with her when they went to talk to Marisol again. *You like punishing yourself, don't you Anderson?*

*

Savannah groaned, staring at the pile of work on her desk. Her to-do list seemed to grow longer every day, and now she had gala tasks to complete. She shouldn't complain. Almost all the tickets were gone. She'd even had the pleasure of adding Will and Denise's names to the guest list.

She longed to call Will, especially since he didn't call like he'd promised. Well…he didn't exactly promise, but she'd hoped he would have called. She wanted to talk to him and not just for silly schoolgirl reasons. She wanted to talk to him about Officer Dunn's news. That news had rattled around in her head for hours. Maybe she could squeeze in five minutes to call him in the afternoon. *Five minutes isn't enough.*

Her intercom buzzed minutes before noon.

"Savannah, your mother is here." Carrie's voice, though bright, brought a weight to the air.

Savannah dropped the folder she held in her hand and lowered her voice. "Is she alone?"

"Yes. Shall I send her back?"

"Yes, thank you."

Within moments, Mama appeared at her door.

"Mama." Savannah stood and smoothed out her skirt. "This is a surprise."

Esther looked around the office before stepping in. "This is a nice place you have."

Savannah fought down a smirk. If only Mama was sincere. "Thank you."

Esther took a seat. "You look busy."

Savannah glanced at all the papers on her desk and resisted the urge to straighten it up. "Things can get very hectic around here."

"Do you have time for lunch? My treat."

This was getting worse. "I'm pretty busy today. Maybe later this week."

Esther let out a loud sigh, her eyes pleading. "Things have been a little strained between us lately. I thought I would do something nice for you."

Savannah suppressed a snort. *Lately.* Things had been strained much longer than that. Savannah tried to figure out how to get out of this tight spot. No matter what Esther did, even her attempts to be nice, left Savannah swimming in guilt. Things had been strained between them because of Esther's behavior. If Savannah said no to lunch, it would be tantamount to refusing Esther's olive branch. Then the strain would be Savannah's fault. "What did you have in mind?"

"It doesn't matter."

Judging by the look in Esther's eye, it did matter. "We can go wherever you want."

Esther smiled and Savannah's dread grew.

Savannah nodded in all the appropriate places in Esther's one-sided conversation during the cab ride. Thankfully it was a short trip to the Beacon House, a café-style restaurant in a historic house in Old Town, Alexandria. Mama chatted along about her life as a governor's wife, not needing much from Savannah to continue.

They entered the restaurant. Patrons filled almost every table. "Maybe we should go somewhere else." Savannah pulled her purse onto her shoulder to keep it from hitting the other people in the crowd around them. If Savannah had thought to drive, she would at least have had the option to leave when she wanted.

"I believe we're next on the list. Let me go check." Esther, in all her commanding glory, marched off to the hostess station. A few minutes passed and Esther hadn't returned. Savannah spotted her on the other side of the waiting area talking on her phone. She abruptly ended the call when Savannah approached.

"It won't be that much longer now."

As if on cue, the hostess called Mom's name.

They were seated near the back of the restaurant, tucked in a corner table. Savannah slid in just enough that she wouldn't be facing her mother. Esther sat with her back to the wall and facing the door.

Esther unfolded her napkin and laid it on her lap. "The food must be great here. It's so crowded."

The waiter came and took their orders. Savannah settled on a grilled chicken salad. It wouldn't be as great as Denise's, but it was probably the best choice after all the fattening food she'd eaten last week.

"Your father is in town." Esther said, rearranging her silverware into a much neater setting than the wait staff had done. "He said you're helping him with some project."

That was the thing about mom. She was never concerned with what Daddy did, just the prestige that came with his job. "I don't know how much help I can give right now."

Esther reached across the table and grasped Savannah's hand. "I'm sure you'll be a great help."

Savannah almost flinched. Touching and giving compliments? Something was up.

The waiter returned with their drinks. As soon as he disappeared, a shadow darkened the table. Savannah looked up and her heart stopped.

Mitch.

He held up his hands in mock surrender. "Before you blame your mother, this was my idea."

"I have to go." Savannah shot up, purse in hand.

Mom grabbed Savannah's wrist. "Please can't we have a civil meal without you always running away? Sit down, honey."

Savannah wavered, heart hammering. If she left, her mother would only set her up again, but she didn't want to be this close to Mitch. He gave Savannah the slightest glare, a look Esther couldn't see.

Cold dread flooded her veins. *He knows.*

"One lunch. Besides, I have some news I think you would want to hear."

Fighting to keep her hands from trembling, Savannah returned to her seat. Mitch sat beside her.

Their food arrived and Mitch ordered a huge meal. Savannah's stomach churned so violently that her food lost its appeal.

"I guess you've been wondering what I'm doing in town." Mitch moved his hands into a steeple. A gesture that annoyed Savannah when they were engaged and still did. "I've been scouting out the area."

Savannah fiddled with her fork. "Scouting?"

"For the best place to rent office space. I've worked out a contract with Domino's Sugar in Baltimore and will be shipping to them."

The room tilted and Savannah squeezed her eyes shut. *No.*

He gave Savannah a pointed look. "I'm going to find a place to live here in the DC metro."

Mom beamed. "Isn't that great, honey?"

Savannah fought back tears.

Her phone vibrated in her purse and Savannah scrambled to get it. She pulled out the phone and saw Will's number on the caller ID. *Thank you, God.*

"Excuse me, I have to take this." She sprang from the table, nearly knocking a waiter over.

She rushed across the dining room and out the front door. "Hello, Will. I need a huge favor. Can you come pick me up?" She blurted out.

A pause. "Are you all right?"

No. "I'm out to lunch with my mother and I need a ride back to the office."

"Where are you?"

She gave him the name of the restaurant and the address. "Could you hurry, please?"

"Are you sure you're all right?" Will's concern sounded in each of his words.

"I'm fine. I just-I need to leave."

"I'm on my way."

*

Will resisted the urge to bust into the restaurant with his badge pinned to his jacket. Savannah's tone had set off alarm bells in his mind. She sounded so…undone. Odd since that contradicted her normal composure. He drove as fast as he could to the address that she'd given him. Thankfully, he'd found a space in front of a meter, a miracle for lunchtime in Old Town. He paid for parking and walked to the restaurant in long strides.

He stepped inside and did a quick scan of the dining room, spotting Savannah near the back. He breezed past the hostess desk and navigated to her. Relief flooded Savannah's face when they made eye contact.

She popped up from the seat, and placed her hand on his chest, just over his heart. A gentle touch, probably to calm him down. It worked.

She turned to the two people seated at the table. "Everyone, this is Will."

Seated at the table was a woman who had to be Savannah's mother. Same color eyes and skin tone but the woman's hair was peppered with grey.

On the other side of the table was a man who set off more alarm bells in Will's head.

"This is my mother Esther and Mitchell Alverez."

Wasn't that the name of Savannah's ex? Will clinched his teeth and tried to smile. Her mother had set her up again.

"Nice to meet you." Will said, shaking Esther's hand. He turned to Mitch, who had already extended his hand.

Mitch gave him a once over. "William."

Will almost laughed as Mitch gave him a firmer than necessary handshake. "No, it's Will."

"Oh." Mitch sat back down.

"Why don't you join us?" Esther put on her best politician's wife smile. "I would love it if you would."

"Actually, Will and I have business we need to discuss," Savannah said before Will could open his mouth.

Esther frowned. "What about your lunch?"

"I'll grab something later." Savannah grabbed her purse and looped her arm around Will's, pulling him close.

Something was really wrong for her to overstep professional bounds. Not that Will minded having her pressed against him.

Will nodded at Esther and then at Mitch. "It was nice to meet you." In a sense it was. Nice to identify the people who could send Savannah into such a panic.

Mitch rose as Savannah stepped away from the table, his nostrils flared.

Will shot him a cool but challenging look, daring Mitch to say something, anything. Will was five inches taller than Mitch and Will made sure to stand straight, adding his height to his intimidation.

Mitch smiled at Savannah. "I'll talk to you later, Ladybug."

Savannah shuddered and gripped Will's arm tighter. "Please don't call me that."

They exited the restaurant in silence, Savannah still clinging to his arm. He led her to his car and opened the door. As soon as they pulled away from the curb, she burst into tears, her sobs so loud Will nearly swerved into another lane. He wanted to question her, but she seemed to need to process her emotions. Thank goodness he remembered that her office was somewhere near Capitol Hill.

Her tears slowed once they crossed into DC.

He shot her a brief glance. "Do you want me to take you home?"

She dug tissues from her purse. "No. I need to go back to the office."

After she gave him the building's address, she said nothing else. Something serious must have happened between her and Mitch for her to react like this. She dried the rest of her tears as they pulled in front of her building.

Will stared at her this time. "Are you sure you don't want to go home?"

She shook her head. "Thank you so much."

She gripped the door handle but then paused, her face laced with confusion. "What did you call me for anyway?"

Despite himself, Will let out a guffaw. Within seconds, they were both laughing so hard that all the tension in the car before evaporated.

"I wanted to see if you wouldn't mind accompanying me to interview Marisol again," Will said between chuckles. "I'm thinking of going tomorrow around two."

"I'm free." Savannah took a deep breath. "You must think I'm crazy."

Will turned to face her, studying her. "I think you are a woman who needs someone to vent to."

Savannah caught the corner of her lip between her teeth and warmth settled in Will's chest. What would she do if he coaxed out that corner of her lip with a series of soft kisses? He blinked a few times, shoving that desire down.

"I--I'm not ready." She looked down at her lap.

To be kissed or to talk? Will reached over and squeezed her hand. "When you are, I'm here."

"Thank you," she said, and to his surprise, leaned over, placed one hand on his cheek and planted a peck on the other.

The softness of her lips and the scent of her rose-scented hair rattled him. His senses teetered on the verge of overload. With a breeze, she hopped out of the car, leaving Will gripping the steering wheel.

Lord, help me.

Chapter 11

It had taken almost five minutes to finish everything she needed to before she could leave with Will. The day had been another busy one, but she'd made sure she'd completed her most important work.

When Savannah rounded Carrie's desk, Will sat in one of the chairs, eyes closed, long legs resting against the side of the small coffee table. She stopped, her stomach doing a slow roll. His relaxed expression highlighted his breathtakingly handsome face. It had been so long since she'd really noticed a man like this. Not since Mitch. Wonder what it would be like to wake him with a kiss.

"Go get 'em, tigress," Carrie said in a low voice.

Savannah shot her a glare. "Stop it."

"We need to talk when you get back."

Savannah ignored Carrie and recomposed herself. She stepped over and touched Will on the shoulder. "Will?"

He jolted upright, stood and straightened his jacket. "Sorry."

She giggled, and then chastised herself. Why did this man make her feel so giddy?

They crossed the lobby and he held the door open for her. As soon as they walked outside, a breeze blew through her hair, pushing it into her face.

"My car is this way," Will said. While she tried to tame her unruly hair, he placed his hand on the small of her back and guided her in the direction of the car. It was a natural touch, but sent heat flaming straight to her face. His hand only remained for a few seconds, but it shook her to her core. He looked straight ahead, shoved his hands in his pockets and seemed not to notice.

He arrived at the car first and opened the door for her. She climbed in his meticulously clean car, which smelled like he'd sprayed his cologne all over the seats. *That beats the new car smell.* He climbed in a few seconds later and she caught a glimpse of muscular thigh straining against the fabric of his pants. She looked away.

"Don't forget your seatbelt."

A hot flush rose to her cheeks. *What is wrong with you, girl?* "Right." She snapped on her seatbelt, wishing she could buckle down her thoughts about the handsome man driving the car.

*

Will had to make small talk. He was totally unprepared for the effect Savannah's nearness had on him. Especially when the wind tossed her hair across her face. It took Superman-strength willpower not to reach over and help her capture the stray strands.

He'd shoved his hands deep in his pockets and gripped his keys until his palms stung. He swallowed hard when she brushed against his shoulder as they walked.

He started the car, pulse pounding. She probably didn't realize it but she was giving him all the right body language. She sat in the passenger seat knees facing him, her legs crossed at her ankles.

He locked his gaze on the road. "Are you doing better than yesterday?" Good thing traffic was light. Being trapped in the car with Savannah for any longer than necessary would be murder on his self-control.

A blush colored her cheeks. "I'm so embarrassed about that."

"Don't be."

She tipped her head toward him. "I normally don't lose control like that."

He dared to steal a glance at her. Their eyes met. Mistake. He gripped the steering wheel, his palms clammy. She quickly looked away from him and out the window.

Why can't you keep your eyes straight ahead? Will snapped his attention back to the road.

They talked about the growing storm clouds and the weather the rest of the ride. Safe subjects. Besides, he needed to prepare to talk to Marisol again. She could hold the key to solving this case.

The nurse greeted Savannah and Will as they approached the station. "Marisol is doing much better now." She turned to face Savannah. "You should have seen her eyes light up when she saw the flowers." Savannah smiled but didn't respond. Did she feel uncomfortable for being recognized for doing something nice? Will knew that feeling.

They walked into Marisol's room. The importance of this interview weighed on Will.

Things started much like the last visit. Except this time, Marisol dark brown eyes were opened and most of the red blotches were gone from her face, some of her beauty restored. Savannah spoke softly in Spanish and the girl nodded a few times. Her eyes nervously went from Savannah to Will and Marisol pulled the coverlet up ever so slightly.

Realization filtered into Will's mind. "She's still afraid of me."

"Unfortunately, yes." Savannah's voice remained soft.

Will shook his head. "Tell her I'm here to help."

"I have. It might help if you relaxed."

Will glanced down at himself. He had absent-mindedly folded his arms across his chest.

"Right." Will quickly unfolded his arms, grabbed the other empty chair and slid it up besides Savannah. He slid his arms from his suit jacket, but when he did, something fluttered out of his pocket, falling on the bed.

The picture of Jordan.

It landed face up on the bed next to Marisol's leg. Time slowed. Will reached for it but so did Marisol. He pulled his hand back. Marisol picked up the picture and studied it. The worn edges testified of how many times he'd pulled it out when he needed encouragement to keep him going. Sometimes Jordan was his only reason.

Marisol's eyes filled with tears and her hand began to tremble. Then, as if her tongue were a newly broken dam, she began to rapidly speak. Savannah translated as quickly as Marisol spoke. Her story was like a script all traffic victims had learned. Marisol paid a Coyote to smuggle her across the US-Mexico boarder to have a better life. She had taken her young son to the Abelua, an older woman who worked for the traffickers, that would "look after" small children while the immigrants worked in the US. Sadly, those children would often be used as leverage to keep them in submission.

Marisol had traveled from Guatemala City to the pick-up point, gave the coyotes 8200 Quetzals and climbed in the back of a false bottom truck. The Coyotes transported her and twenty-five other girls across the border where they were taken straight to the house that was raided in DC, only stopping briefly to let them out of the false bottom.

Will watched Marisol's reaction to each of his question as Savannah translated. Some she answered quickly. Others, tears formed in her eyes and several moments would pass before she would speak. She answered like a woman who had been shamed and victimized. A brave victim, nonetheless.

Will studied Marisol, worried that she may not hold up much longer. "Does she know the other girls?"

Marisol shook her head after Savannah finished speaking.

Will braced himself and reached for the sketch from Grant. He already knew who the man was. He prayed Marisol could add some personal info to his knowledge, but things might not go as he wished. Seeing someone from the house may send her back into a state of fear. "Ask her would she mind looking at the sketch for me?"

Savannah relayed the question. Will noticed the girl's brave face fade slightly just for a moment.

"*Sí.*" Her breath had become more laborious and her eyelids dropped. But she still held the picture of Jordan.

Will fought to keep his emotions in check. She'd left Guatemala and suffered great tragedy for her son. She could have died but that danger paled in comparison to her love for her child.

Will often faced one question once people found out that Will worked with traffic victims. They would ask why would someone put herself in such danger. There were many answers to that question, but Will understood Marisol's answer well. For the love of a child. Some of these women only wanted to give their children a better life. He sympathized because he might have done exactly what Marisol had done…if not more.

*

Savannah watched the scene unfolding in front of her. Will had gotten Marisol to open up…but he had closed down the minute Marisol lifted the picture from the bed. Savannah only got a brief look at the picture, but it was a child. Who could it be and why did it have such and impact on Will and Marisol?

Marisol shuddered when Will showed her the drawing from the sketch artist. She gripped Savannah's hand with one hand and Will's picture in the other.

"This is the coyote." Marisol's fear sounded on each word.

Savannah translated to Will, who looked almost as uncomfortable as Marisol. Several notches of his controlled demeanor disappeared when the picture had fluttered to the bed. As much as she wanted to question him about the picture, she focused on Marisol.

She listened as the girl told her how she'd paid the man in the picture to bring her into the country. Savannah glanced at her and then to the sketch.

All the sound in the room muted as her vision narrowed on the face on the page.

She knew this man.

She discreetly leaned closer, stealing another glance at the sketch.

Where do I know him? Maybe he was from another case she'd worked. She'd seen her share of criminals.

"Savannah." Will's voice jolted her. He wore a puzzled expression. "Can you ask her if she knows his real name?"

Savannah turned to Marisol. "Do you know his name?" A valid question but a long shot. If Marisol had a name for him, it was probably an alias.

Marisol shook her head. "He didn't give me his name."

Savannah relayed Marisol's answer and Will let out a deep sigh, his frustration simmering just under the surface. She checked her own frustration. Maybe if Marisol had given a name, it might have jogged her memory.

Will gently took the sketch back from Marisol. "Thank you."

Marisol managed a weak smile.

"You did great." Savannah patted Marisol's hand.

Marisol looked down at the picture of the child again. "You think the boss man wants his son back? Can I have him?"

Son? Savannah glanced at Will, certain he had no idea what Marisol was asking. "She wants to know if she can keep the picture."

Will clinched his jaw and gripped his knees. "She can keep it. I have plenty more." His voice oozed thick with emotion despite his attempt to sound casual.

Savannah gave him a curious look and he looked away from her gaze. Savannah relayed his words, and for the first time since they'd met, Marisol looked…happy was too strong a word. She looked peaceful.

"Gracias," she said.

Will shifted in his seat. "You're welcome."

Marisol clutched the picture to her chest. Savannah watched Will closely. His shoulders tensed.

A nurse came into the room to check on Marisol.

"Are you almost done? She needs to rest." Her polite but firm tone sent a clear message that it was time for them to leave.

Savannah and Will rose from their chairs and exited while the nurse began to check Marisol's vitals. Maybe she would work up enough courage to ask about the boy on the ride home.

*

Will rolled his shoulders as he and Savannah walked to his car. Why did he feel like he'd gotten into of a street fight?

Because of Jordan.

Dark clouds had muted out the day's remaining sunlight by the time they reached the parking lot. Jordan held such a prevalent place in his thoughts to the point he only briefly noticed that he and Savannah were back in the parking lot where the shooting had occurred.

Savannah pulled her coat closed. "Looks like the rain will start before we get back."

"Yeah." Will hurried to open her door, pondering the weird bond Marisol formed with the picture of Jordan. It was hard to watch the way she'd cradled the picture. He understood her pain. Longing to hold your child but not being able to, for whatever reason. He wanted to tell her that he would do everything he could to find her child and the man in the drawing. He didn't. Better to show her.

The short drive from the hospital across New York Avenue quickly turned into gridlock.

"Traffic around here is crazy," Savannah said from the seat beside him. "This is worse than Atlanta traffic."

"It's not normally this bad. Looks like we're going to be stuck for a while."

"There is no other way to go?" Savannah asked.

"Not really. Our only other option is to go somewhere and wait it out."

"Go back to the hospital?"

"No. We could get some dinner and get back on the road once rush hour is over." Will held his breath. "Are you hungry?"

"I am. That would certainly beat sitting in the car."

Will merged over and exited at Rhode Island Avenue.

He glanced over at Savannah. "Do you eat sushi?"

"I love sushi!" Savannah clapped her hands. "I used to eat it all the time in Georgia but I haven't found a place to get it other than my local supermarket. I still feel like I'm new to town."

"I have the perfect place to take you." He whipped the car and headed up Eastern Avenue. The traffic flowed a little smoother. The ride to Matuba Sushi restaurant in Silver Spring took less than twenty minutes.

"Looks like we made it just in time for dinner." Savannah pointed to the hours of operation sign on the door. Will swung the door open and let her go first. They were seated at a table in the corner. A cozy corner.

Savannah called her office and informed them that she wouldn't be back in the office for the day.

The waitress appeared in no time with glasses of water.

"Do you need more time to look over the menu?"

"No," Savannah said.

"Yes," Will said at the same time. She giggled and Will drank in the way her eyes sparkled.

"I didn't think you would be ready that fast."

"I know what I want." She took a sip of her water.

I like that in a woman. "Most women take forever to decide. Guess I'm the one who needs hurrying."

"No, take your time. Not like I have somewhere else to be."

They both ordered Sushi and Savannah ordered hot tea and Wonton soup along with her order.

"I never knew this place was so close." Savannah looked around the room. She rubbed her arms and Will noticed the goose bumps forming there.

"Take my jacket." Will shrugged out of his jacket and handed it to her. She hesitated in taking it. He shook it at her. "It's not going to bite you."

"Thank you." She slipped her petite arms through the sleeves and the jacket swallowed her.

Since they'd both ordered sushi, the dish arrived on one long plate. Will volunteered to bless the food. He prayed a simple prayer, including Marisol in it. He secretly prayed for God to help him through this dinner with Savannah sitting across from him. She gave him a strange look after he was done.

"Is something wrong?" Will asked.

"No. I- no."

Will watched her unwrap her chopsticks and begin eating. Will dipped his roll in the Wasabi sauce that accompanied it, scooping up a healthy portion. Her mouth gaped open.

He shrugged. "I like spicy food."

"I would have never guessed."

"Why?"

Savannah's face flushed pink. "You seem like you like things simple and uncomplicated."

"You're saying I'm boring."

"No, you seem so…"

"Uptight?"

Savannah waved her hand. "Never mind."

Will chuckled. "Don't let the law enforcement façade fool you. I'm a ball of complications."

Savannah paused. "Like the picture of the little boy?"

Will nearly choked. He'd walked right into that one.

Savannah gazed at him. "Is that your son?"

"Yes." Will inhaled. "Actually, no. Not anymore."

His heart warmed at the compassion in her eyes. No wonder she was so good at her job. She could melt the hardest hearts with that gaze.

"Did he die?"

"No. His mother and I…" *How could he explain this?*

"Oh, I understand."

No you don't, but whatever you think is probably better than my explanation. "I doubt it. I still don't understand." He shrugged, trying to look casual, but Savannah still watched him closely.

Will put his chopsticks down. "Jordan was never my son. I just didn't know it."

She waited. Even though he realized she was treating him like a victim, it worked. Compassion softened her face.

"While I lived in Baltimore, I had a relationship with his mother. She got pregnant. I took responsibility for my actions and tried to be a good father. Jordan was another reason I took a job in DC. Shantel already lived here and I wanted to be closer to them."

Savannah pulled his jacket tighter around her shoulders. "If you don't want to talk about it, you don't have to."

Will took a deep breath. The idea of unburdening his soul to her held such appeal. "Two months ago, Jordan was playing at school and fell off the monkey bars. When he did, he cut a deep laceration in his knee and lost a lot of blood." Will shuddered at the memory. "He had to have surgery to close the artery and the hospital asked if Shantel and I would give blood just in case."

Will took a sip of his water and continued. "When we did, the lab informed us that neither of us was a suitable match."

"And that made you wonder."

Will nodded. "So while my son had surgery, I had a paternity test done."

"I'm so sorry, Will." She reached across the table and grasped his hand.

"So am I. Six years, I've raised Jordan like he was mine."

"Do you think Shantel knew?"

"I don't know what I think. She neglected to tell me she was intimate with someone else while we were dating. That betrayal was nothing to the pain of giving Jordan up to his real father."

Savannah squeezed his fingers. "You can still be in his life."

Will shook his head. "Now you sound like my mother."

"She's right."

"That will just complicate things. We decided it was best not to tell him yet. He's too young to understand." Will chuckled. "Actually, he's very bright so he might understand."

"How are you going to live in the same city with him and stay away?"

"I'm transferring to one of the California field offices in fifty-seven days." He closely watched her facial expression and noted the disappointment there. "Besides, it's not fair to his real father."

"I'm sorry to bring up such a painful subject. I could tell you were struggling when Marisol asked to keep the picture."

"I guess she and I have something in common."

*

Savannah fought the urge to hug Will. What a horrible story. His love for Jordan was evident but yet he had no rights to him. Will slid his hand away from Savannah's and she instantly missed the warmth of his fingers against hers. Oh, how she longed to comfort him.

Just then a loud rumble of thunder resounded from outside. They both glanced up at the ceiling.

Savannah frowned. "That sounds bad."

"Maybe we should go." Will motioned for the waiter.

Savannah reached for her wallet and Will shot her a stern look. "Don't even think about it." He placed his credit card in the bill holder and the waiter hurried off.

"I can pay for my own food."

"Don't bother arguing with me. My mother raised a gentleman."

Savannah stifled a grin. A stubborn gentleman. The waiter returned and Will quickly signed the bill, but not quick enough. Rain had already started to coat the front window.

"I'll go get the car."

Savannah opened her mouth to tell him not to, but he gave her another glare, the message clear. She chuckled and held up her hands. "I'll wait for you here."

She watched him trot through the rain and tried to remember the last time a man treated her like this. Not just paying for the food, but doing everything he could to protect her and make her comfortable. Too bad his transfer would happen in fifty-seven days.

The ride home didn't take as long as she expected. Will talked a little but remained mostly focused on the crazy drivers on the road. As they crossed the Maryland state line into DC, the rain lessened. This was perfect weather to curl up and watch a movie. Maybe she would pick up some ice cream on her way…

She groaned. "I didn't drive to work today. Can you drop me off at the nearest Metro station?"

"How about I take you home?"

Savannah shook her head. "I don't want to inconvenience you by making you drive all the way to Virginia."

Will gazed at her, half smile on his face. "I live in Virginia."

More time in the car with Will worked for her. "Okay."

They rode through DC, the thwack of the windshield wipers keeping the beat. As they arrived at her apartment, the rain increased to a steady patter. They gave themselves a three count and sprinted to the awning above the front door of her building. Running through the rain made her feel like she was seventeen again and on her first date. Of course, this date turned out better but it wasn't a date. Not really.

She couldn't remember the last time she'd felt this at ease. Will's presence, the rumble of his laughter, his grin or his intense attention, relaxed her like a day at the spa. She grinned at him as he wiped droplets of water from his face.

"You didn't get too wet, did you?"

She lifted her arms. "No, but I'm afraid your jacket did."

"It will be fine." He studied her, his gaze so intense she could almost feel it pressing against her skin. "I guess you better get inside before you catch a cold."

She shrugged out of the jacket. "I'll take this to the dry cleaners and get it back to you."

"You don't have to. I'll have to put these slacks in, too." His lifted his leg a little to reveal his soaked, grimy pant cuff.

Savannah giggled. "I'm sorry."

Will reached for the jacket. "Nothing the cleaners can't fix."

Savannah pulled it away. "No, I insist."

"Savannah, I'll put them in the cleaners together."

Her cheeks warmed at the sound of her first name on his lips. She eluded him again when he reached for the jacket.

He frowned. "Give me the jacket so you can get inside."

"I'm going to put this jacket in the cleaners for you." Savannah straightened her shoulders. "My mother raised a lady."

A smile played at the corners of his mouth. "I'm sure she did, but it will be easier if I put the whole suit in the cleaners together."

Savannah still held the jacket behind her.

He shook his head. "You're going to make this difficult for yourself."

In one fluid movement, he grabbed her around her waist with his right arm, arching her body into his. He grabbed the jacket with his other hand. She yelped and tried to pull away.

"I spend my day catching people," he said with a laugh.

She took note of how well his suit camouflaged his muscular physic. "No fair." Savannah pulled at the jacket but Will held on. His grip around her waist was firm but not tight enough to hurt her. As a matter of fact, it comforted her. She felt safe.

This is the way love is supposed to feel, capturing and freeing at the same time.

She stopped and looked up at him. His smile slowly faded to an intense gaze.

"You should get inside." His voice rumbled deeper than normal. His gaze searched her face, lingering on her lips. Her heart hammered, but she didn't want to pull away.

Slowly, he lowered his mouth to hers.

She forgot about the cold spray of rain on her feet. His kiss was almost chaste. He hesitated at first, and then stepped closer, his body shielding her from the chill of the air. The rest of the world faded. The moment dwarfed all her worries about her mother, Mitch, her tears over trafficking victims. The only thing she knew was the peace that came with being safe and wanted.

She wrapped her free arm around Will's shoulders, rose to her tiptoes and kissed him back with bravado. Will let out a soft groan and pulled away, his expression as shell-shocked as she felt.

"I should go."

She nodded, almost breathless.

"Good night." He trotted down the stairs. The rain instantly dotted his shirt.

"You forgot your jacket," Savannah whispered as she watched him climb into his car.

Chapter 12

If Carrie thought Savannah smiled more before she had dinner with Will and his mother… Savannah went through the day grinning, especially when Carrie questioned her about her light mood. No matter how much she questioned, Savannah refused to tell her about her kiss, and the subsequent phone calls they'd shared over the weekend. Did she even have the words to explain to Carrie all that had happened in those three short days? She found it hard to believe herself.

All of her wondering about Will's interest in her were banished with that kiss. She'd never seen him as unraveled as she had during their phone calls. He seemed almost…nervous. She could almost hear him blushing through the phone. Unfortunately, each phone call highlighted the fact that he would be transferring soon, but nothing was stopping her from enjoying every minute with him.

She caught herself humming as she went from her desk to Carrie's. She even laughed at Carrie's frustration at being unable to extract any information from her as they took a coffee break.

She thought of the feel of Will's lips on hers as she left Carrie and walked down the hall to her office. She would eventually tell Carrie what happened after she enjoyed keeping her in suspense.

Halfway there, she noticed movement in her office. Not uncommon for her employees to get files from her office. She stepped to the door and a familiar scent wafted to her: Mitch's cologne. She froze, but before she could turn and go back down the hall, he appeared in the doorway.

His smile chilled her. "I didn't think you were going to come back, Ladybug."

"Please stop calling me that."

He motioned her inside, like it was his office and not hers. "I'm sorry but it fits you so well. Sweet fragile Ladybug."

Sweat beaded around her hairline. "What are you doing here?"

"I was in the area. Thought I'd stop by and invite you to coffee or dinner."

She sat her coffee on the desk and then fisted her hands. A surge of boldness welled up in her. "Mitch, I don't want coffee, lunch, dinner or anything with you. We're done and it's time you figured that out."

Mitch's eyebrows rose and he stepped closer. "You almost said that like you meant it."

She moved away from him, putting the desk between them. "I do mean it."

Mitch chuckled and sank into one of her chairs. "You know, I can remember a time when you said you'd love me forever."

That's before I found out that you're a monster. The words danced on her lips and she ground her teeth together to keep them in.

Mitch stared at her. "All I want to know is what happened. One minute, we're making wedding plans, looking at invitations, and the next, you've moved up here to get away from me."

Savannah's stomach heaved at his reference to the invitations. She shook her head, driving back the memories. "I can't believe you expected me to still marry you after you were investigated by the FBI."

Mitch sat up straight. "They found nothing, but you didn't even stick around until the investigation was over. You left, and rather suddenly."

Savannah swallowed. "Mitch, it's been a year. I've moved on. I think you should, too."

He sat back, smugness in his expression. "Did you move on with that FBI agent?"

A flash of anger ignited in her. "What difference does it make to you? We're done and nothing's going to change that."

Mitch sprang from his seat, and in seconds was behind the desk, beside her. He grabbed her arm. Savannah let out a yelp and Mitch tightened his hold.

"Shh. I don't want anyone to think I'm hurting you."

Fear numbed her muscles as her heart hammered. She pulled away from him. He moved his hand but grabbed her around her waist.

"One day you're going to realize how much I love you." His breath warmed her cheek. "What I am willing to do to have you back."

She fought the urge to hyperventilate. "Does that include shooting out my windows?" She blurted out the words before she could consider what she was saying. "Or maybe shooting out the windows was your back-up plan after the shooting at the hospital failed."

Mitch leaned back, shock coloring his expression. "What?"

"Don't act surprised. Maybe all this was just to get me to run back into your arms, but it's not going to happen."

Mitch touched her face. His eyes held something that looked like love. "Savannah, you should know I would never hurt you. I hope you believe me."

Savannah seized the opportunity his confusion provided to put some distance between them. She stepped away. "Hard to do when you've been nearly stalking me since you got to town."

Mitch flashed her a grin that spread over his whole face. "Not stalking. I only want to talk to you. We have unfinished business between us."

Savannah panted. *He knows. He has to.* Her mouth worked to respond, but no words came.

The sound of someone clearing their throat echoed through the room. Carrie stood at the door, her expression like stone. "Sorry to interrupt, but I wanted to know if you wanted me to contact Mr. Christopher or were you going to do it?"

Savannah exhaled hard. Mr. Christopher was their code word for the police. They'd developed it once when a former trafficker showed up at the office threatening to kill them all.

Did she need the police? What would she tell them? The truth? "No, I'll contact him later. Could you show Mitch out? I'd appreciate it."

Carrie rolled her eyes at him. "Right this way."

Mitch followed and Savannah's shoulders slumped with relief. He turned and glanced at her.

"You'll be seeing me around."

Savannah flopped down in the chair. What was she going to do about him? The urge to unburden her soul brought tears to her eyes. If she did, she would be exposed for the hypocrite she was, not to mention putting herself in more danger. What would Will think of her? He'd spent the better part of his adult life fighting the same kinds of people as Mitch. A person Savannah had chosen, even if through omission, to protect.

She rested her elbows in her desk and willed her heartbeat to slow. *What do I do, Lord?*

She sat back in her chair, taking in the clutter on her desk.

Wait. Clutter? She had partially cleared her desk before she'd left to get coffee. Her desk may not have been clean, but it wasn't as disorganized as this.

Carrie came through the door. "Boss, I'm so sorry. I didn't know he was back here."

"Did you see anyone else come into my office while I was gone?"

Carrie frowned. "No. Who was that guy?"

"My ex-fiancé, Mitchell Alverez."

Carrie folded her arms. "I'll keep my eye out for that one."

Savannah stared at her desk. Why on earth would Mitch have gone through her things? She took a deep breath. She had no idea what he could be looking for, but whatever it was, Mitch probably wasn't going to go away until he found it.

*

If someone had studied Will's demeanor upon arriving at work, they would have thought he'd lost a loved one, not gotten a girlfriend. He trudged to his desk, and dropped down in his chair hard enough to push it backwards. He removed his jacket and memories of the last time he'd seen Savannah filled his mind. He didn't need another person complicating his emotions. He'd unburdened his situation with Jordan to her way too easily. He'd kissed her…like a girlfriend.

Maybe girlfriend wasn't the best word, but how else would he describe her? He wanted her to be his girlfriend. His heart even held a hint of wanting her to be something more. He couldn't do that, no matter how strong the desire. Besides, he hadn't been in a relationship for so long that he'd grown rusty. What did women expect out of relationships these days? He was sure Savannah didn't want to be dating a man halfway across the country.

Will's cell rang, and he braced himself for another completely mushy but disarming conversation with Savannah. He steeled himself. He couldn't let his emotions run away with him like all the times he'd talked to her this weekend.

When he read the caller ID, he groaned. Shantel. And to think he'd been complaining about talking to Savannah.

"Hello?"

"Hey Will, it's Shantel." Her voice sounded casual, like she had made a normal social call.

Will gritted his teeth. "Where have you been? Did you know that I had to get Jordan from school last week?"

"I knew he was with you." Her whiny tone riled his anger.

"What do you mean you knew he was with me? You didn't check your messages or answer your phone."

"I knew you would take care of him." Her voice wavered a little bit. Will's anger checked a bit and a sliver of guilt entered his mind. He hadn't asked if she was all right or what had happened.

"Shantel, you know I don't mind taking care of Jordan, but I thought we agreed that it would be best if I stayed out of his life."

"Yeah, that's what we agreed." She paused. "I'm not so sure that's a good arrangement."

Will leaned way back in the chair as her words flooded him with both joy and dread. Could she really mean it? He would take her up in a heartbeat. She could also be up to another one of her games. "Why do you say that?"

"I'm not sure I can do this. Jordan loves you so much. He's miserable. And Derrick…" Will heard her sigh. "Derrick is Derrick. This is all so hard."

Will wanted to yell at her, but kept his tone level. "This is hard on all of us. You can't keep jerking Jordan around or me for that matter. You have to make a decision and stick to it. For Jordan's sake."

"You were such a great father," she said almost as an afterthought.

Will clenched his fist. "Shantel, don't do this."

"I just wish things had turned out different. I wish Jordan never fell. Then we wouldn't know."

Will's anger returned with a vengeance. "You wish Jordan never fell? How about wishing you never cheated on me!"

Shantel let out a loud huff. "I don't even know why I called you. I never get any sympathy from you, Mr. Perfect, self-righteous FBI agent!"

"You don't need sympathy. You need to own up to what you did. You ruined my life and your son's life. You can't shift that blame to anyone else."

"It's a wonder you don't get a nosebleed from looking down at people all the time. Just once I'd like to see you get knocked off your high horse." Shantel spat back.

"I'm hanging up. When you are ready to be civil, call me back." He jabbed the *End* button on the phone and dropped it so hard on the desk that the sound reverberated around the room. Some of the agents stopped and stared at him. He took two deep breaths. How dare she blame him for her stupid mistake? He'd never leave Jordan at school. He'd taken good care of this kid that wasn't even his. She wanted to blame him for her horrible parenting?

Will stormed back and forth in the small space behind his chair. His desk phone rang. *Probably Shantel again.* He braced himself for another fight.

"Will Anderson."

Instead of Shantel, another voice filled his ear. A deep voice with a heavy accent. "Agent Anderson. I guess being shot isn't enough to keep you away from crime-fighting."

Will stood, shock trickling from his mind down to his toes. *The man from the house.* "I've recovered. How's your leg?"

The man laughed. "Touché. I must admit I was surprised you hit me. You're a good shot."

"Not as good as I would like."

"You managed to hit me in the dark. Others can't hit a near stationary target in a well-lit parking garage. Give yourself some credit."

"Why don't you tell me where you are? I'll come right over and I'll even give you another head start."

The man laughed again. "You're quite impressive but I wonder how your bravado would hold up if something bad happened to someone you loved."

Will gripped the phone receiver. "I don't think you'd have to worry about my bravado. You would be worried about yours."

"Think you're above pain, Agent Anderson? You have no idea of the pain that comes when your loved ones are hurt. Like if your mother died a martyr like your father. What about your little boy?"

Will's heart pounded. "Unfortunately for you, I would channel all my pain into finding you and making sure you spend the rest of your life miserable."

"You've already done that, Agent Anderson. I'm only returning the favor and I will be very generous."

A flash of anger burned through Will. This small talk wasn't very helpful and clearly he needed to find this guy as soon as possible. What he could discern was that he wasn't dealing with any ordinary criminal. Most of them wouldn't threaten an FBI agent. He had to get some meaningful info out of this guy. "It's only a matter of time before I find you."

"You won't catch me. You didn't last time."

Last time. "You didn't threaten my family last time."

"As delightful as this conversation is, I must go. I have things to attend to."

"I'll see you soon."

The man laughed. "Maybe I'll see you first."

The phone clicked and the call ended.

Will stood, receiver in his hand, not moving. His mind kicked into high gear. He mentally reviewed everything the man had said, scrutinizing each thing even though he could get a recording of the call from the cybercrime division.

This guy has some guts to call here. Will put the receiver down and picked up a pen, grabbed a note pad and started to write. His mind wanted to dwell on the fact that the man threatened Jordan and his mother, but he turned it to the highlights of the conversation.

Maybe he should focus on the threat. The man made this personal, which meant their first interaction was personal. He picked up a pen and a notepad. *Call Zach and have him narrow the search of the Baltimore cases to ones involving angry family members who were also suspects.*

Will rose from his desk. He needed to fill Carter in on this. He turned to leave as the man's words him popped into his head.

I guess being shot isn't enough to keep you away from crime-fighting.

His arm was injured in the shooting, not in the house raid. His suspect had also made reference to the parking garage. The man knew about the shooting, but Carter had said he'd kept Will's name out of the news. So how did know, unless…

Will restrained himself from running but went to Agent Carter's office as fast as he could.

Carter turned from a file cabinet as Will knocked on the doorframe. He frowned. "What's up? Is your son okay?"

Will's heart tripped. *That creep threatened Jordan.* "I just got a call from our suspect from the house raid."

Carter looked up, mouth half hanging. "Are you serious?"

He recounted the phone call. "His little threat gave me a few clues to his identity."

"I'm more concerned that he knew about the shooting. That information wasn't released to the public." Carter rubbed his face. "Makes me wonder if he might be involved."

Will's suspicions were about the same. "He didn't say enough for me to be sure."

"Call in an order for a recording of the phone call."

"I will."

"I can't believe he actually called you." Carter picked up the phone and began dialing. "I'm ordering security on your mother and your son."

"Thank you."

Will returned to his desk, his emotions further stretched than when he talked to Shantel. As much as she infuriated him, he was glad she hadn't taken his name off Jordan's records. The threat from his suspect made it clear that Will needed to keep access to Jordan until this case was solved.

Chapter 13

Savannah hadn't heard from Will in twenty-four hours and she was acting like she was still in high school, waiting with both anticipation and worry. Each time she found herself checking her phone, she scolded herself. *I am a grown woman and he is a grown man.* They both had busy lives that could keep them from talking for longer than that. That didn't mean anything.

Still, she fought the urge to call him. She had plenty of legitimate reasons to reach out to him. She hadn't told him about the fact that her windows had been shot out, not broken. She even considered telling him about Mitch being in her office. Despite that, she restrained. She didn't need to appear too eager or desperate.

Unfortunately, the day dragged by without hearing his voice. By the afternoon, she'd decided she would call him as soon as she got home...and then promptly decided to go leave early. She almost accomplished her plan, but Carrie brought her more gala work, which kept her even later. Night had fallen by the time she shut off the lights in her office.

She gathered her things and went to Carrie's desk. "You heading out?"

Carrie shook her head. "Not yet. The FedEx man is running late and I have to get these tickets for the gala out today."

Savannah sighed. "All right. Don't stay too late."

Savannah fished out her keys and her phone as she traversed through the parking lot to her rental. A habit she'd developed after the shooting at the hospital parking lot. She remembered how she and Will had joked about bad things happening in parking lots. Fortunately, the only bad thing was driving that rental even longer.

"I can't wait to get my car back," she said aloud.

The sound of her words hadn't left the air when she heard another sound.

Footsteps.

She half-turned, but a hand clamped down hard over her mouth, crushing her lip against her teeth. A big hand. She still managed to let out a strangled cry.

Strong arms wrapped around her and pulled her backwards. Her phone and keys clattered to the ground. The heel of her shoes scraped the ground as she tried to twist from the grasp.

The arms tightened and a man grunted. He pulled harder. Savannah screamed against his hand and pushed her shoulders backwards hard.

The man pressed his lips to her ear. "Did you think you could get away from what happened?"

Oh, God. She screamed again for no one but the man to hear.

"You did good to keep your mouth shut, but I can't afford for you to have a change of heart and start talking to your FBI boyfriend." Even through the haze of her terror, the voice, thick with a Hispanic accent, sounded familiar. He yanked her hard this time, pulling her off her feet. Both cold and heat flushed her. The chill of fear and the heat of survival. She tried to scramble away and he heaved her hard, dragging her several feet away from her car.

She heard a door open behind her. *I'm being kidnapped.* The words fluttered from her subconscious with such clarity that she screamed again. Something wild erupted in her. Her instinct to escape kicked into high gear. With new fervor, she fought. She wrapped her leg around the man's, causing him to stumble. She shifted her head enough to catch a sliver of the skin on the man's finger between her teeth and bit down hard.

The man yelled, then swore, his grip loosening.

"Stop! Police!" Another voice echoed to her ears and she saw an officer running toward them.

Senses heightened, she brought her heel down on the man's instep, bringing a howl from him. The man released her and she tumbled to the ground, scraping her knee. She tried to call out to the officer, but they man's grip must have been tighter than she realized. Her ribs ached as if they were compacted.

She scooted forward to find safety before the man tried to grab her again, but it wasn't necessary. The man, who wore a black ski mask, jumped into a car that sat just behind him. The door slammed and the car sped away.

The officer reached her. He helped her off the ground. "You all right, ma'am?"

Savannah opened her mouth to speak, but she sobbed instead.

*

It had been along time since Will had worked this hard on a case and it felt good. It felt even better that Carter hadn't pulled him off the case, something Will had worried he would do. His boss hadn't and Will had dove into finding this guy. He couldn't deny the fact that Jordan being threatened added to his fervor.

His newfound busyness had, however an unfortunate side effect: he hadn't had a chance to call Savannah. It hadn't been long since they'd increased their phone calls, but he'd quickly grown used to hearing from her often. Dangerous, but wonderful.

For all his hard work, he hadn't moved any further along on his case. Once he'd obtained a warrant for the phone call, the phone company had sent him the call info. Of course, the call was made from an unregistered cell phone, one that would not be tracked easily. He'd sent out the sketch to the local police departments and even to the local hospitals in hopes the man had sought professional treatment for his gunshot wound.

He picked up the phone and dialed Zach. His friend answered on the third ring. "Hey, Zach. This is Will."

"Anderson. You must have read my mind. I'd planned to call you today, not that I have good news."

"Can I assume you didn't find anything?"

"Nothing that stands out. I only had time for a quick glance."

"Maybe I can help narrow your search. Look for cases where a male family member was also suspected of a crime."

"Hmm. That's an interesting angle I wouldn't have thought of."

"Me, either. Luckily my suspect let it slip." Will paused. "Can you move this up on your list of favors? The suspect threatened my family."

Zach whistled. "That's pretty serious. I'll see if I can find a desk sergeant to help me out."

"Thanks, man."

"You got it."

Will returned the receiver to the base and looked over all the paperwork on his desk. He'd done all he could. Now more waiting. He found himself staring at his desk phone every few minutes, willing it to ring.

To his surprise, it did ring. He snatched the receiver up. "Agent Anderson."

"Agent Anderson, my name is Carrie Boone." Her voice held an unsettling warble. "I'm Savannah Elliott's administrative assistant."

Dread tightened his chest. "Is Savannah all right?"

"Yes. Well, no." Carrie sighed. "Someone tried to kidnap her in the office parking lot. She managed to get away unharmed, but she asked me to call you."

Will sprang from his chair. "I'm on my way."

He ran down to his car and sped to Plateau. His mind twisted from anger to alarm as he thought of Savannah being attacked. He pulled into the parking garage, only to find police cars blocking the entrance. He flagged a cop down. "I need to get in there."

The cop gave him a wry look. "I'm sorry but—"

Will held up his badge. "My--my girlfriend was attacked."

The cop moved aside and directed Will to park near the front entrance. Will climbed out of the car and ran up the aisle. It didn't register that he had no idea where he was going until he saw Savannah standing in a huddle of police officers including Officer Dunn. Carrie stood at Savannah's side. Savannah spotted him, pushed through the crowd, ran to Will and then threw herself into his arms.

She buried her face in his chest. "Will." She let out a heart-breaking sob.

He pulled her close, pressing his face into her hair. "It's okay. I'm here."

He held her as she cried, wishing he could somehow completely envelope her, protect her from any other harm. He let his heart go free for the few minutes they stood together and allowed himself to feel how much he cared for her. He kissed her forehead.

After her tears slowed, Will moved back, righting her...and his own emotions. "Are you hurt?"

Savannah shook her head. "No." She looked up at her, eyes filled with fear. "I didn't even get to see his face."

Will glanced over her shoulder and found Officer Dunn watching them. "Have they finished interviewing you?"

"They took an initial statement. Officer Dunn decided to wait once I told her you were coming."

Will wrapped his arm around Savannah's waist and led her back to the group.

Officer Dunn stepped forward, thumbs hooked on the belt of her holster. To Will's surprise, she'd lost her casual and easy demeanor. "I need to talk to you both. Can we go to your office, Ms. Elliott?"

Carrie led the way as the four of them walked in silence up to Savannah's office. "I'll call your brother." Carrie detoured to her desk and picked up her phone.

"Thank you."

Will slid his arm around her waist again. Once her brother arrived, Will would have to abdicate his position to him, but he would hold on as long as he could.

*

Leaving Carrie at her desk, Savannah led Will and Officer Dunn to her office. Unable to take another step, she sank into the first seat. Her fear levels waned and physical and emotional exhaustion weighed her every movement. Will stood behind her chair like a sentinel.

Officer Dunn remained by the door. "This case is getting pretty serious. I know you two have told me everything, but I want to go over it again."

Will retold his account of the shooting. Savannah reasserted that she hadn't seen that much.

Officer Dunn let out a frustrated sigh. "Ms. Elliott, can you think of anyone who would shoot out your windows and then try and kidnap you?"

Will shifted to face her with a scowl. "Shoot out your windows?"

"Yes. I thought she would have told you." Officer Dunn looked from Savannah to Will. "We determined that Ms. Elliott's windows were not broken. We recovered brass. We're running it."

Will and Officer Dunn's attention returned to her, their faces holding the expectation of an answer.

"I can't think of anyone." *No one but Mitch.* She averted her eyes at the thought. As much as his actions were creeping her out at the moment, she didn't believe he was involved. He'd said he still loved her, and even in his twisted mind, he probably did. She couldn't deny that he genuinely looked shocked when she told him about the shooting and the broken windows. Besides, if he wanted to kidnap her, he'd had plenty of opportunities before tonight.

Officer Dunn studied her. "I'm sure you've made some enemies in this line of work. Maybe you had trouble with a trafficker you've come across. Did the guy who tried to grab you seem familiar?"

Savannah swallowed. "As a matter of fact, his voice did."

Officer Dunn pulled out her notepad. "What did he sound like?"

Savannah forced herself to replay the sound of his voice. "He had a very heavy Latino accent." She looked at Will. "He mentioned you. He said he didn't want me talking to my FBI boyfriend." She shifted in her seat to hide her discomfort at the man's exact words. *It was good that you kept your mouth shut...*

She battled with herself. She should probably tell Will and Officer Grant all the man said, but that meant telling them what she'd kept her mouth shut about. Shame choked out her words. She couldn't tell them especially since she didn't really know for sure that the man was referring to the night in the warehouse.

At her words, Will jolted like someone had pinched him. Was he opposed to being called her boyfriend?

He moved to crouch in front of her. "Do you know where you heard the man's voice?"

"No."

Will placed his hand on hers. "Do you think you would remember it if you heard it again?"

Savannah closed her eyes and remembered the words. She shuddered and wrapped her arms around herself. "I think so."

Will stood. "Can I use your computer?"

Savannah motioned him to it, both she and Officer Dunn wearing the same confused expression. He went to work tapping on the computer, a look of concentration knitting his brow.

He looked up from the screen. "Listen to this."

Savannah listened as what sounded like a recorded phone call that started with Will's voice.

When the caller's voice followed, Savannah shivered. "That's him."

Will held up his hand. "Listen to the whole thing."

The recording continued and Savannah's horror grew, not just from hearing her attacker's voice, but also from what he was saying to Will. Threatening Denise and Jordan.

By the time it ended, Savannah's heart pounded in her chest. "I'm pretty certain that's him."

Officer Dunn stepped closer to Will. "Okay. Who was that?"

Will sighed and ran his hand over his face. "The suspect that I told you about. The one who threatened me."

Savannah frowned at Will. "He's threatened you before?"

Will nodded. "He called me yesterday with the new threat. I thought it was a little bit of a coincidence that someone with a heavy Latino accent would be threatening me and trying to kidnap you."

Savannah fought back tears. "Could it be the same man?" If it was, he didn't sound like someone she wanted to tangle with. As much as she didn't want to accept that it was the same man, the look that passed between Officer Dunn and Will told her that they believed it.

Officer Dunn put her notepad in her pocket. "I think we need to look at all of the cases you two have worked together."

Will let out a short laugh. "That will be easy. It's just this one."

Savannah's shoulders slumped. "I haven't done anything in this case that would warrant someone wanting to hurt me."

Officer Dunn placed a hand on Savannah's arm. "I know it seems like a stretch, but we need to explore every lead, even the smallest ones."

Savannah dropped her head, exhaustion fogging her thoughts.

Will rose from the chair. "You should get home."

Savannah put up no resistance to the idea. She followed Will back to the parking lot like a lamb. She didn't even protest when he offered to follow her home. As she drove, her brain kept trying to fit the pieces together. Her emotions, on the other hand, shot from one place to another. She went from fear, to gratitude for Officer Dunn putting patrols outside her building to—she sighed. She didn't want to admit it, but feelings strong enough to be considered love for Will swirled in the mix.

You're emotional, Savannah. You can't be in love. If she were, this would be a horrible time to admit it. That didn't, however, change the fact that knowing Will was only a few cars behind her soothed her aching heart.

Chapter 14

Will marveled at the stark contrast between his life now compared to just a few weeks ago. Before, his only worry was how fast he could transfer, now…now he had more complications than he could deal with. Was there ever a time when both his person life and professional life held so many unanswered questions?

What was the caller's connection with Savannah? Savannah seemed to react better than he had when she identified the caller as her kidnapper. Although Will had controlled his outward response, inside a storm had erupted. He wanted to find this guy and make good on his promise of a do-over.

Despite his anger, this new development stumped him. Other than Marisol's case, Will and Savannah had nothing else in common other except for their new personal connection. What did the man not want Savannah to discuss with him? He would have to find all this out somehow, definitely before someone made another attempt on Savannah.

He'd followed her home that night, wanting so badly to be in the car with her. Her strength surprised him again. That she could hold it together and drive herself home was a testament to it or to the fact that she was in shock. He couldn't tell which had carried her home last night, but he was glad that she made it there safely.

Will hadn't slept well. Giving up, he'd dressed and went into the office early. Most of the cubicles were empty this time of morning and he was glad for it. He needed to think for a moment. He didn't want to cause any problems between the FBI and MPD, but he needed to take the lead on this. Well, he wanted to take the lead. Carter might have kept on him the case after the threat, but he might pull him after he found out about Savannah's kidnapping attempt and the fact that the two cases were connected.

Maybe he could convince Carter to form a taskforce of sorts, comprised of Will, Officer Dunn, and as much as he disliked the man, Officer Grant. That would at least keep Will in the loop and give Carter some assurances that Will wouldn't be running the case off his emotions.

He checked the clock. Officer Dunn had mentioned that she would send over all her case notes on the kidnapping. That gave him a little while to review his notes and get a cup of coffee. He rose but his cell phone ringing brought him to a halt.

"Will Anderson."

"Anderson, this is Officer Dunn. Where are you?"

Anderson? "I'm at the office."

"I need you to meet me." She rattled off an address before Will could grab a pen. Half her words were swallowed up by the sound of the wind in her phone but he caught the address, all he needed. "How fast can you get here?"

Will frowned and studied the address. It was in SE. "In traffic, maybe a half an hour."

"Get here quick."

Will ended the call and rushed toward the door, the oddness of the call motivating him. As he reached the hallway to the break room, he detoured. He would probably need that cup of coffee.

The wind had picked up considerably by the time Will crossed the 14th Street Bridge in SE. Traffic delayed him only five extra minutes, a miracle. He didn't have to check the address for the location Dunn had given him. Police cars blocked off an alleyway between two sets of row houses.

Will pulled his car up close to the other cars and climbed out. The wind whipped the tails of his jacket around and he wished for a heavier coat. Officer Dunn stood near the opening of the alley giving one of the other officers instructions.

Will stepped beside her. "What's all this?"

She huffed and shook her head. "A mess. Come with me."

She led Will behind the police tape. The narrow space blocked out some of the sunlight and gave the impression that Will had stepped inside. When his eyes adjusted to the change in lighting, he saw the mess Officer Dunn referred to.

The alley was littered with six bodies covered in sheets. They lay sprawled about one hundred feet away from the mouth of the alley.

Will took in the scene. The shell cases, still on the ground, were already chalked and marked with numbered tents beside them. The first shell lay closer to the opening of the alley than the victims and the same with the second. That meant someone came into the alley and opened fire on everyone there. He looked at the bodies. Although they were covered, some had an arm or leg almost casually stuck out from under the sheets. The position of those limbs confirmed Will's suspicion. Most of the bodies were facedown, which means they were shot in the back.

Officer Dunn looked at him. "We responded to reports of a shootout and sent some officers over and found this." She motioned to the bodies laying closest to where she stood. "These two we know, but I was wondering if you might be able to identify some of the others." She stepped over one body.

Will frowned. "Why me?"

"We found a Crown Vic fitting the description you gave parked in the back of the alley, right down to the flat tire. We'll take a look at it after this."

Will followed close behind her. Finding the shooters would be a boon for the case, but Will didn't want to find them like this.

She lifted the first sheet.

"No."

Then the next. Will shook his head as he stooped to study the man's face.

She and Will followed that pattern, Dunn lifting the sheets and Will not recognizing the poor souls that lay beneath.

They were down to the last two bodies. They lay face up. Dunn sighed. *She's about as hopeful as I am.* Will's thoughts shifted when he spotted the face of the man from the shooting with a bullet hole in the center of his forehead.

"That's one of them."

That added energy to their movements and they hastened to the last body. Dunn lifted the sheet and stared at Will.

Another bullethole to the head. "That's the driver."

She dropped the sheet. "Are you sure?"

He nodded.

She folded her arms across her chest and scowled. "I was hoping it wasn't them. Can't question dead bodies."

"Don't give up hope yet. There still may be some evidence in the car."

They rounded the corner and walked to where the Crown Vic sat with the doors opened. Officers milled around the car and Will and Dunn joined them.

One of the officers popped the trunk and let out a whistle. "Come look at this."

Will moved to the trunk and peered in. It was loaded with high-powered assault weapons.

Officer Dunn shook her head. "What in the world?" She turned to the other officer. "Get these down to the lab and get it processed as fast as they can."

She looked at Will. "Please tell me you have some theory that will shed some light on our cases. It could be a simple gun sale gone bad and no help to us."

The two shooters from the hospital dead and the only ones face-up. Will shook his head. "I don't think so." He turned and headed back to the alley where the bodies lay. "Do you notice anything?"

Dunn stared. Will saw her eyes going from one spot to the next. "Seems like the shooting started down there." She pointed to the opening to the alleyway.

"Right." Will took a step closer to the last two bodies. "These two are face up when the others are face down."

Dunn rubbed her hand over her eyes. "Which means that the others were probably running away."

"But not these guys."

"Why weren't they running?"

"I suspect they knew whoever it was."

Dunn stared at Will. "I don't know. That's a bit of a stretch."

"Then why do these two have bullet holes to the head and not the others? Seems a little personal to me."

Dunn sighed. "Okay. Say you're right. That still leaves us with no answers."

Will let his arms fall. "That's true."

Dunn shifted. "I guess all our hopes are on the content of the car. I'll send over info on whatever I find when I get back into the station."

Will nodded and trekked back through the grime of the alleyway back to his car. His mind whirled as he passed the line of bodies. Dunn's informants had maintained that someone still wanted he or Savannah dead. Could this shooting be because the two suspects failed? How did Savannah fit into all this? One thing he knew for sure: the brothel house was the center of it all.

Chapter 15

Savannah awoke to sunshine on Sunday. To her eyes, the light seemed extra bright. The past two days seemed like the darkest of nights. She'd stayed holed up in her apartment with only Will, Josh, Dawn and Mama as visitors. Josh, Dawn and Mama had come over Saturday morning. Will visited Saturday night. Her family had stayed longer than Will, and she secretly wished it were the other way around. Will brought a sense of security, something she desperately needed. After the drama filled angst her mother brought, she longed for Will's cool levelheadedness.

He had assured her that MPD and the FBI were working hard to find who tried to kidnap her. It also comforted her to see the gleam of determination in his eyes. He had suggested that she go to a safe house or maybe leave town for a few days, but that would be impossible with the gala coming. Besides, she knew full well that running didn't necessarily mean she'd escaped her problems. If only she could.

She'd slept well past ten, the first night of any sleep she'd had since the kidnapping attempt. Unfortunately, it was troubled sleep. She kept hearing the voice of the man from the kidnapping in her head. *It's good that you kept your mouth shut.* Was it really good? It couldn't be if people were trying to kidnap her despite her silence. *It would be good to tell someone.* She shuddered at that thought, but an unmistakable desire to share her secret pulled at her emotions. At least then she would be free, despite anyone's reactions.

She shuffled into the kitchen for a late breakfast feeling like she'd stayed up all night. Her cell phone rang as she started her coffee pot. She hoped to see Will's number, but still brightened when she saw it was Josh instead.

"Good morning."

"Hey, baby sis. How are you doing?"

"As good as can be expected."

"Any news on the case?"

Savannah sat at the small dinette set near her kitchen. "No. Will assured me that they are investigating every lead."

"They will be turning over every rock and beating every bush once Dad gets done with them."

As alarming as her kidnapping attempt was, she left it to Josh and Mama to inform Daddy. She didn't want to have to listen to him scold her about not taking his help in the first place. "I'm sure."

"Speaking of Daddy, he's coming for dinner tonight and wanted to know if you were coming."

Savannah let out a sigh. "I don't feel up to it."

"Come on, Savannah. Even if you don't come for Daddy, come for Dawn and I. I'm worried about you. You need to get out of the house."

I'm safe in the house. "I don't know."

"Call your FBI boyfriend and ask him to escort you."

Savannah's face heated. "Will is not my boyfriend."

"Sure." Josh laughed. "Call him whatever, but come."

Savannah rested her head on her hands. Will had assured her that it was safe to go out. Not only that, she didn't want whoever tried to kidnap her to think she was afraid. "I'll be there."

"Great."

She ended the call and second-guessed herself. She might be able to fool her attackers, but fear settled deep in her bones.

*

Will needed to go to church. He needed divine help on the confusing tangle of cases consuming his life. He would wear sackcloth and ashes if he needed to in order to feel some sort of peace. If church would give him that, he would go and go early. It had to help. He dressed, twice making sure that he had replaced the picture of Jordan in his pocket, and drove to the church without calling his mother. His attendance would be a nice surprise.

As the sun began to add an orange glow to the trees, his mind began to settle. His spirit, however, stirred beyond his mind's grasp. It was a sensation that he hadn't experienced in a while. A strange kind of anticipation . . . of what, though? He honed his mind in on the feeling. By the time he pulled into the church parking lot, his heart thumped in his chest like he was going in to do a raid.

He found his mother sitting toward the middle of the sanctuary.

Mom rose and kissed him on the cheek. "Hi, sweetie. I didn't know you were coming today."

"I needed to be here." He took the seat beside her.

She smiled at him. "How is Savannah?"

Will shot her a sidelong glance. "Doing well."

Mom shifted to face him. A ray of colored sunlight flashed through the windows at the front of the church and caught the edge of her hat. "I like her. You should invite her over again."

Will clenched his jaw shut.

Mom folded her hands on her Bible. "Do you like her?"

"Yes, mom."

"She's an amazing woman."

"Mom—" His phone buzzed at his side. The ID read Alexandria PD. He groaned. That call meant work on Sunday. "I need to get this." He unclipped the phone, rose and exited the sanctuary before his mother could respond. "Agent Anderson."

"Good morning, Agent Anderson. This is Detective Branch from Alexandria PD. I've located someone who fits the description of a suspect you're looking for."

Will pressed the phone to his ear as the choir began the opening hymn. "From a sketch?"

"Yes."

Will looked toward the hallway that led to children's church. "Do you have him in custody?"

"You could say that, if you consider being examined by the coroner as custody."

Will blew out a breath. "Where are you?"

Detective Branch gave him the address to the Lucky Motel on Route 1.

"I'll be there in twenty minutes."

He glanced toward the sanctuary. The peace he needed was so close, but it might as well be miles away. He sent his mother a text message that he wasn't coming back. She wouldn't be happy since she probably had many more Savannah questions for him.

The Lucky Motel sat about a mile away from the I-95 exit. Around it sat two other hotels, neither of them in better condition than the Lucky. If this was his guy, this would turn the case in a direction he didn't want it to go: another dead end.

The motel's tiny parking lot had law enforcement cars occupying almost every parking space. Will clipped his badge on his belt buckle and joined the crowd of police milling around the door of unit number nine.

"Agent Anderson?" A stocky, almost ebony toned man stood just inside the doorway. "Detective Branch."

Detective Branch gave Will a quick handshake and led him into the room. A man lay sprawled face down on the floor, hands bound behind his back. The back of his head was nothing more than a bloody mush. His right arm was tattooed all the way up to his chest. Will let out a huff of air.

Detective Branch stepped beside Will. "ME thinks he could have been dead for 12 hours, but he'll know more once they do the autopsy."

Will stepped gingerly around the bed. Everything else in the room looked normal. A skewed bedspread was the only possible sign of a struggle. Will glanced back at the door. The lock didn't look damaged. Will squatted and got a closer look at the man, leaning back on his heels. It would have been great to catch this guy alive. If someone went through the trouble of killing him meant he knew something the killer didn't want anyone else to know. He was a loose end.

"There's something else." Detective Branch led Will outside. Will shielded his eyes from the bright sunshine.

"We started a canvas of all the people on the hotel guest list. No one was supposed to be in this room." He stopped in front of number ten. "One of the officers saw the curtains move and heard sounds from inside."

He opened the door and stepped back for Will to enter.

Five frightened Latino women in various stages of nakedness turned their faces toward him, the lesser-clothed ones wrapped in blankets. Two uniformed officers were in the process of taking their statements.

"None of them have passports. They're not talking much either." Branch folded his arms. "One of them could probably give us the time of death."

This was probably what happened to Marisol. Will let out a huff. "Does this place have security cameras?"

"Yes, but they were all conveniently pointed in the wrong direction. Maybe the owner. . . " Branch flipped through a notebook, ". . . a Mr. Todd James, knows something."

Will stepped out of the room. "He better know how he has possibly trafficked girls in a room that's supposed to be empty."

Branch motioned Will toward the rental office. The officer posted at the door stepped aside when Will and Detective Branch entered the room. The hotel owner, a white haired man possibly in his 50's, sat in a low chair behind the desk, looking as frightened as the girls from the room.

Good. A little fear of law enforcement could go a long way.

"Mr. James, I'm Special Agent Anderson from the FBI—" Will moved his jacket aside to expose his badge.

"FBI?" The man's voice cracked.

Will leaned on the edge of the desk. "How did the girls get into the room?"

Mr. James looked away. "I don't know."

"Were you here last night? Who gave them a key?"

"I told them everything I know." He pointed toward the officers. "I heard some gunshots so I dialed 911. That's it."

"Did you see a car leave the parking lot?"

"No. I was on the phone with you guys."

"So you don't know how those girls got into the room?" Will leaned forward.

"I told you I don't."

Why did they always have to lie? Will scowled. "When did the man in room nine check in?"

"About eleven last night."

"Do you normally have guests check in at that hour?"

"People stop in all hours of the night. Wanna get off the road and rest a bit. Not unusual."

"Did he have reservations?"

Mr. James paled a few shades. "I don't know."

Branch moved toward the desk and picked up what looked like an old school reservation book. "Let's find out then."

Will traced his finger down the guest list. He stopped when he saw room number nine. The name read Pablo Valedez. "Our friend had reservations. How did he make them?"

Mr. James clamped his mouth shut and stared out the window.

"Hey!" Will pounded his hand on the desk, sending a waterfall of papers over the side of the desk. Mr. James jumped and clutched the front of his shirt.

Will lowered his voice. "How did he make the reservations?"

The man started rocking slowly back and forth. "You don't understand."

Detective Branch eased forward. "Help us understand."

"He said if I talked, I would be killed."

"Who said that?"

Mr. James dropped his head. "Pablo. The guy in nine." He looked up at Will, eyes pleading. "You gotta protect me. He's going to kill me."

"Well, he's dead. If I were you, I'd be more worried about whoever killed him. Tell me how he got the girls here."

Mr. James rested his head in his hands. "He would come about once a month. Each time he would put the girls in an extra room."

Will folded his arms. "Where was he from?"

Mr. James trembled. "I don't know."

"You still haven't told us how they make the reservations."

"Through a travel agency. They call a week before they come and reserve a room."

"And you give them two?" Detective Branch asked.

"Come on," Mr. James whined. "I didn't know what they were doing. They told me all I needed to do was give them an extra room and they would pay me a grand a night. I gave them the keys and looked the other way."

"I want the name of the agency." Will left him to shuffle through some papers on his desk. Detective Branch fell in step beside him.

"So?"

"I think he knew exactly what was going on in his motel," Will said.

Will jogged to his car and retrieved a copy of the sketch of Juan. He brought it back to the office. Will placed the sketch in front of the man. His eyes grew wide.

"Just to be sure, is this the man in room nine?"

"Yeah, that's him."

"What kind of vehicle does he drive?"

"White truck. One of those ones stores use to make deliveries."

Will frowned, mind reviewing all the vehicles in the parking lot. "Where's his truck?"

Mr. James shrugged.

Will turned to the officer at the door. "Take him into custody."

Detective Branch hooked his thumbs in his belt and nodded at Will. "Is this your case now?"

Will bit back a snort. "It seems to be connected to something I'm working on. You guys keep working and keep me posted. Let me know if you find that truck."

Will climbed back into his car and closed the door. The quiet of the car mimicked the peace he longed to feel. The view in front of him, however, evaporated any hope he had of settling his nerves. The paramedics arrived, heading straight to unit 10. The girls would be checked out and then taken to a transitional house. At least these girls looked healthy. Finding where they came from would be easier than his attempts with Marisol.

He fished out his notepad and wrote down all he'd learned from the hotel owner. He also jotted down some questions. He knew where Pablo was now. That question was answered, but was only to be replaced by so many more. *Who killed Pablo? Where is the white box truck now? How did the travel agency tie in, if it did at all?* He let out a deep breath. He felt like he was no closer to the end of this trail of crime than when he first talked to Marisol, but he had to be getting closer. He had plenty of pieces to this puzzle. He just couldn't see how they all fit together.

There was one bright point in all this. Will would be able to tell Marisol that the man she so feared wouldn't be bothering her anymore.

Chapter 16

A gleaming, black Lincoln Town Car sat in Josh's driveway. Daddy's car. For as long as she'd remembered, big shiny, black cars were her father's preferred method of travel, each one bigger than the last. Although not a limo, sitting in the back of those cars made her feel like a child sitting in a grown-up's seat. Especially when Daddy's large life sucked her in. She parked behind it, alarm and surprise filling her mind. He'd beat her to the house. Daddy liked to make an entrance as much as Mama did. His early arrival didn't bode well.

Dawn must have been watching from the window because she swung the door open before Savannah could get out of her car. She wore a panicked look. "You're here."

Savannah rushed through the doorway checking her watch. It read 6:52pm. "Am I late?"

"No, but your father was about to send out the hunting hounds for you."

"I'm not a child anymore," Savannah muttered.

Dawn laughed. "Watching your family's dynamic never ceases to amaze me."

Daddy sat at the head of the dining room table. Hard to believe she hadn't seen Daddy in person in over a year. He'd aged but in a way that made men look more distinguished. He had lost some weight. Even so, he still had an impressive stature. His temples had gone completely white and his face was laced with weathered lines of what could be mistaken as wisdom.

Daddy stood. "Princess." He pulled her into a hug, smothering her with his cologne-doused shirt.

"Hi, Daddy."

He released her and gave her the once-over. "You look great. DC has been good to you."

Esther snorted from behind her.

"Thanks." Savannah reached up and fingered his new gray streak. "Looks like Georgia hasn't been good to you."

He chuckled. "The voters like it."

"That's all that matters," Josh quipped. Being the dysfunctional family they were, no one replied to his remark.

They sat and Daddy started dinner immediately, without grace. Her parents' relationship with God greatly depended on who was watching. Jesus was a political asset, not their personal savior. Savannah offered up a prayer of thanks, as did Josh and Dawn.

"So how is the gala planning going?" Daddy dished way more than the recommended serving of mashed potatoes on his plate.

Savannah took the bowl of string beans from her mother. "I'm almost sold out of tickets. I'm thinking of calling the Gaylord to see if I can get a bigger room. I doubt it though."

Daddy cut into his meatloaf. "I'll call over there."

Savannah grimaced. "You don't need to. I can handle it."

"I'm sure you can but sometimes it takes a little clout to get things done." He stared at Savannah. "I'm sure they'll find you a bigger room if the governor of Georgia asked them to."

Anger boiled in her but she kept it contained. "I can handle it. Besides, you're not involved at all. They probably wouldn't talk to you."

Josh smiled at her. "Savannah has some clout of her own. Maybe as much as you have. Did you see her on BET?"

Savannah shot Josh a look. One she'd given him often. Things were already tense and he had a bad habit of trying to put their father in his place.

Her father, seemingly unaffected by Josh's jab, turned his attention to Savannah. "I heard it was good."

So you didn't watch it. "Ticket sales increased quite a bit after that news story."

Her father nodded. "That's good."

They finished their meal making mostly small talk. Dawn's pregnancy seemed to be the most comfortable topic. Once the conversation waned, Savannah gathered her dishes and rose.

"Savannah, have you heard from the police about the kidnapping?" Daddy wiped his mouth with a napkin.

"I had an update over the weekend. They're working hard on the evidence they have."

Mama clutched her napkin. "I can't believe someone would be so brazen. Something like this would never happen in Georgia."

Savannah bit back a laugh. "Things like that happen all the time in Georgia, Mama."

She wrinkled her nose. "At least you would be near family if it did."

Savannah motioned to Josh. "I am near family."

"Josh has his own family to look after," Mama continued. "If you were back home, you would have someone to watch you specifically. Protect you."

"I agree with your mother." Daddy laid the napkin beside his plate. "I happen to know one young man that would love to watch after you."

Savannah's stomach turned at the knowing smile her father gave her. "Daddy. . ."

Her father held up his hand. "Mitch seems to be a nice young man. I don't understand why you have refused him. He has the resources to keep you safe."

"What I don't understand is why you and Mama won't leave this alone. Mitch and I are done."

A flicker of anger found its way into her thoughts.

"I've been shot at and someone has tried to kidnap me and all you two are worried about is hooking me up with Mitch." Her voice rose as she spoke, bringing looks of alarm from everyone at the table.

Daddy frowned. "I am concerned about you. I'm just trying to make sure you're happy and safe. Mitch can do that for you."

Josh leaned forward. "Daddy, Savannah's in a relationship."

Daddy let out a sharp laugh. "With the FBI agent she nearly got shot with? I wouldn't call that a great start to a relationship."

Dawn rose from the table. "Would anyone like dessert?"

Although Savannah saw through Dawn's ploy, she was happy that it worked. Mama even offered to help Dawn serve cake to the guests. Her father attempted to engage Josh in conversation, but Josh's eyes stayed focused on Savannah. So intense was his stare that Savannah wondered if he could see the tears forming in her eyes.

Her parents pushed her on Mitch and accused Will of being dangerous. Only if they knew that it was the other way around.

Chapter 17

Savannah massaged her temples. She looked at the gala spreadsheet again but still didn't see it. She had seen the police car parked outside her building when she left in the morning and the one patrolling the parking lot when she arrived at Plateau. She had complete faith in MPD and Will's ability to find whoever was behind this whole mess, but the wait grated her nerves. She needed a break from the pressure.

Dinner with her family the night before certainly didn't help. She wanted to hold on to her anger at her parents about pushing a relationship with Mitch, but she couldn't blame them. They didn't know who he was or what he'd done. She hadn't told them, and if she had her choice, she would never tell them. Revealing Mitch's secret would be revealing her own. That she had once been a coward and protected herself over others.

Her shame blanketed her and she turned her focus back to the spreadsheet. This fundraising gala would help those in need. She would make sure it was a success.

As she typed, one of Carrie's favorite euphemisms filled her mind: *Doing the right thing for the wrong reason still makes it wrong.* Savannah dropped her head. The truth of that statement could be applied to everything she'd done in the past year. Her whole organization was built on her attempts to ease her own guilt. *This is all selfish. Maybe that's why I'm having all these troubles.*

She shook her head, surprised at the emotional toll her thoughts had on her. After the past two weeks she'd had, she didn't need to add such weighty things to her mind. She needed to do something relaxing to take her mind off her problems.

Savannah collected her things and walked to the front desk. "Carrie, I think I'm going home early."

Carrie gave her a surprised look. "Sure, boss. Anything I can finish for you?"

"Nope. Everything on my desk can be handled tomorrow."

"All right. Have a good night."

"That was exactly what I plan to do."

She got to her car, walking quickly and scrutinizing the parking lot a little more than normal. Once out of the lot, her mind drifted to what a relaxing evening would consist of. Maybe a good dinner and a movie.

She let out a groan. In all the excitement of the past couple of days, she hadn't gone grocery shopping. Fear had kept her in the house.

She detoured from her route home and headed to the grocery store. *A quick trip and I'll be home curled up in front of the sofa in no time.* She wandered to the pre-made meals, roaming up and down the aisles like a homeless person. Maybe she could skip dinner and go straight to bed. Her stomach protested at that thought. Nothing in the pre-made meals section looked particularly interesting until she spotted the sushi and smiled.

Will and sushi were now synonymous.

He hadn't called since Sunday night after she'd arrived home from Josh's. He hadn't shared good news. The two shooters had been found dead in DC and the man who he believed tried to kidnap her was found dead in Alexandria. The revelation didn't lower her anxiety levels. They still didn't know why any of this was happening. Will had tried to comfort her the best he could, but she could sense his frustration.

Maybe he needs a relaxing evening, too. She dialed his number.

"Hello."

Just the sound of his voice brought a full grin to her face. "Hi, Will."

"Hi, Savannah." His mellow voice soothed her nerves even more. "What's up?"

"I'm standing here in the supermarket looking at some sushi that I'm sure aren't as good as the ones we ate."

"Yeah, good sushi is hard to find. You're having sushi for dinner?"

"I guess so. I don't have any food in my house and I'm trying to decide what I want to eat."

"How about some grilled turkey chops with risotto and broccoli?"

"That's sounds wonderful. Where can I get that?"

Will laughed. "That's what I'm making for dinner tonight."

"You cook?"

"You don't?"

It was Savannah's turn to laugh. "Not really. And you know how bad that is for a southern woman."

"I don't know how you managed."

"I stayed out of the kitchen." Savannah remembered the days she'd volunteered to help with her father's campaign to avoid helping Mama in the kitchen. It wasn't that she didn't want to learn to cook. She needed to stay out of her mother's path more than she needed culinary skills.

"Why don't you come over for dinner? I always cook enough for two."

"Are you just saying that?"

"No, I used to be a dad, remember?"

She winced. "Right. In that case, I would love to join you."

Will rattled off directions to his house, which wasn't far from the grocery store. "Dinner will be ready by the time you get here."

"Can I bring something?"

"Maybe dessert. I'm all out of ice cream."

"All right. See you soon."

As she selected an apple pie from the prebaked items, she caught a glimpse of her reflection in the glass. She straightened her hair then caught herself. *What are you doing going to his house? Call him back and tell him you changed your mind.* The only problem with that is she couldn't think of another place she'd like to be right now.

*

Thank goodness for comp days. Having Savannah over for dinner was a wonderful reward for having to work Sunday.

Will frantically set the table and managed to set up two candles before sprinting into the bedroom to change. He struggled to find an outfit good enough for company but not too put together. He wanted to keep things casual. It had been six years since he dated. After his relationship with Shantel, he'd taken dating more seriously, which caused him to date less. Were he and Savannah really dating? Maybe that was something they could clear up tonight.

The doorbell rang as soon as he removed the risotto from the heat. He surveyed the room once more. He opened the door and Savannah stood smiling wide, looking breathtakingly beautiful.

She must have come straight from work, dressed in a black suit. It appeared the day had taken a toll on her ponytailed hair. A few wispy locks had escaped and framed her face.

Will stepped back and waved her inside. "Welcome."

She held the pie out in front of her. "I brought a pie. I hope you like apple."

He helped her remove her coat with one hand and took the pie with the other. "That's perfect. Have a seat at the table and I'll put this in the kitchen."

From the kitchen's look-through window, he watched her casual inspection of the place before she sat down at the table.

"Nice house."

"You know anyone who would want to buy it?" Will called out, and then regretted it. He didn't want to seem too happy about transferring.

If she had taken his comment the wrong way, her expression never betrayed it. "I've always wanted to own a home but I've always been a little afraid of having such a big space for only me. I guess I'll wait until I have a family."

With all that compassion, Savannah would make a great mom. He could easily imagine her raising a full brood of kids.

Will didn't respond and began serving the food on the plates. She came to stand beside him as he did. He watched her carry them to the table. He sat down and noticed the glasses he'd placed before she arrived.

He frowned. "All I have to drink is orange juice."

Savannah giggled. "That will be fine."

Once Will had poured the juice in their glasses, Savannah offered to pray. As she did, he realized he'd never once prayed with Shantel. Grace or anything else but he had prayed with Savannah three times. Some Christian he was. Shantel probably could have benefited from a dose of faith.

Savannah sampled the risotto. She covered her mouth with her delicate fingers. "This is delicious," she cooed. "I'm so jealous. I never learned to cook anything beyond the basics."

"I can teach you how to make it if you like."

"No, you can cook it for me."

"I'll have to air mail it to you from California." Will said and watched a frown form on Savannah's face. *Don't talk about the transfer.*

"I forgot."

Will, after scolding himself about the topic of conversation so far, dug into his food. He found himself fighting a grin at Savannah's reaction to the rest of the meal. Even though she ate in slow measured bites, she finished everything on her plate. "You have a healthy appetite."

"It's a genetic trait for southern women. We may be dainty, but we can eat any man under a table. Especially when the food is as incredible as this."

Will let out the grin he'd been holding. "I'll keep that in mind."

"I guess great cooking runs in your family." Savannah rose and reached for his dishes. "Thank you so much for inviting me."

He frowned at her, keeping his grasp on his plate. "What are you doing?"

"I'm going to wash the dishes." She tugged at the plate.

He still didn't release it. "I'll put them in the dishwasher."

Savannah gave him the same glare he'd given her when they'd had sushi.

Will guffawed. "Okay, okay. I know. Your mother raised a lady."

She floated off to the kitchen. He watched her, which was very easy to do. She looked perfectly at home in his kitchen. His stomach sank. Why couldn't this be his reality?

*

Savannah fought the feeling of this being a normal evening shared with her boyfriend. Will had promised to stay out of her way as she cleaned the kitchen, but ended up standing over her shoulder, directing her to all she needed to get the dishes done. The conversation between them flowed even though tension constricted most topics, especially ones involving the future. Will managed to throw in a comment about his transfer to California in every topic. Like he was reminding her. Or himself.

"You ready for pie?" Savannah put the last pot in the drying rack.

Will chuckled. "Oh, no. I'm stuffed. Aren't you?"

Savannah flashed him a sly smile. "I always have space for dessert."

"I can't eat anything else. How about a movie?"

Savannah smiled. If she didn't know better, she would think this was a real date.

Will led the way back to the living room. Savannah sat down on the couch and took off her shoes. She tucked her knees under her while Will called out names of the movies he owned. None of them interested her, but she enjoyed Will's detailed synopsis of each movie.

"I'm sorry, Will. I don't watch movies too often. Why don't you pick?"

Will decided on something called *Bourne Identity*, he assured her it was the first of three great movies. He sat down beside her, his nearness instantly warming her. She swallowed hard. The feeling of comfort she got from sitting near him alarmed her, reminding her how tightly bottled her emotions concerning men had been for the past year. Mama's words rang true. She hadn't made any attempts to date since Mitch.

Here she sat with Will, who slid his arm along the back of the chair as the credits began. Such a casual movement but it sent her emotions zinging off the walls of her heart. She tried to focus on the movie but it proved challenging with Will slowly inching toward her. She tilted her head to look him in his eyes.

"You're supposed to be watching the movie." Her voice came out in a whisper, all she could manage with him so close.

"I've seen it before." He reached up and caught a stray lock of her hair.

She quirked her lips, and his gaze instantly shifted to her mouth. Her heart did a little shimmy. "So watching me is more interesting?"

Will's expression turned thoughtful. "Actually, I was thinking that kissing you would be even more interesting."

Savannah moistened her lips. "Is that the wisest thing to do?"

He moved within inches. "Don't know. But it will be interesting." His warm breath tickled her lips. She tipped her chin slightly, a subtle invitation. The boldness of her act left her feeling airy and disembodied, but it only lasted a second. Will's lips met hers, grounding her.

The kiss held such longing, almost like he was searching for something only found on her lips. She reached up and pressed her hand against his cheek. Her heart rate zipped faster, her pulse thumping against her neck. Will leaned closer and curled his arm around her.

A loud knock at the door jolted them both.

A rush of relief flooded her mind. Any longer and things would have definitely gotten more heated than they needed to be. Will glanced at the door and then at the clock on the wall and frowned.

He rose from the couch. "I'll be right back," he said over his shoulder.

Savannah watched his demeanor change as he approached the door, the most serious she'd seen him all night. He checked the peephole and stiffened. He swung open the door and there stood an African-American woman with horribly blond, closely cropped hair and a little boy who Savannah instantly recognized as the boy from the picture. Jordan.

"Shantel," Will said, his voice pinched.

Tears streaked down both Shantel's and Jordan's cheeks. "Take him."

"What?" Will closed the door a little, blocking Savannah's view of the woman. She could still see Jordan.

"Just take him. I can't do this anymore. You love him. You take him!"

Savannah watched the little boy. He hadn't moved since Will opened the door. His shoulders were hunched like the backpack he wore weighed a thousand pounds.

"Jordan." Will stooped down to eye level with him. "Go inside while your mom and I talk."

Jordan trudged in the door, and then caught sight of Savannah. He paused, a slightly surprised look on his face. She rose from the couch and approached Jordan.

"Hi, Jordan. My name is Savannah. Let me help you with your jacket."

He eyed her a little longer, but didn't refuse her help. He shrugged off his backpack and Savannah placed it beside the couch. He peeled out of his jacket. They both sat on the sofa in silence. Savannah took a deep breath. Although their conversation was muffled, the tenseness of Will and Shantel's tones wasn't.

Jordan sniffled and wiped his face with the back of his hand. "Are you my dad's girlfriend?"

"Uh…" Savannah tried to hide her surprise.

"Does my dad like you?"

He still called Will dad. Savannah's heart shattered a little more. "Yes, I think so."

Jordan folded his hands in his lap and sighed.

"Are you hungry, honey?" Good thing she'd helped with the dishes. She'd packed up more than enough food to feed Jordan.

He shook his head. "We had McDonald's on the way over."

"How about some warm milk?"

He didn't make eye contact. "No thanks. Where are you from? You have a nice voice."

Savannah smiled. "I'm from Georgia. It's below South Carolina. As a matter of fact, I'm named after a city in Georgia."

Jordan looked up at her with tears filling his eyes again. "I'm from Washington, DC. I think I was named after a basketball player. Does that make me special?"

His words seared her heart. "Oh, honey. You don't have to be named after someplace or someone famous to be special." Savannah wiped his tears with her thumb but fresh ones quickly replaced them. She pulled him closer and his crying turned to hiccupping.

"If I was more special, my dad wouldn't leave and my mom would love me." He put his arms around her waist and held on for dear life. It took all her strength not to join in his sobbing. Such a heavy heart for such a little boy.

After a few minutes, Jordan's sobbing slowed and his breathing turned even. Savannah glanced at the door. She could still hear Shantel's and Will's muffled voices. Situations like these didn't have clear answers. It only left brokenhearted people in its wake.

*

"Shantel, you can't just drop Jordan off every time you have a crisis." Will tried to stifle his voice but it still came out like a boom in the quiet night air.

"You keep him. He wants to be with you. You are what's best for him."

Shantel turned toward her car, but Will grabbed her arm. "He's not my son. I don't have any legal right to keep him."

"Your name is still on the birth certificate."

Will folded his arms across his chest. "What about Derrick? Where is he?"

Shantel looked down at her shoes, her shoulders heaving. "I don't know."

"What do you mean you don't know?"

"He left."

Will anger kicked into high gear. "So this is about your boyfriend leaving you, not about being a fit mother for Jordan."

"I don't know why I expected you to understand. You are the perfect parent."

"What do you think this is going to do to him? Knowing you don't want him?"

"He knows I love him." Shantel stormed off and climbed into her car. She sped off, leaving Will standing in his driveway. The night had turned chilly but his anger insolated him from the cold. If he had gotten a case like this at work, he would have called CPS immediately and reported Shantel for abandonment. Then the Department of Social Services would come and collect Jordan. That wasn't going to happen. Maybe he would give her a few hours to come to her senses.

Will stepped into his living room to see Jordan sleeping soundly, curled up in Savannah's lap. She looked up at him with such sadness in her eyes. Savannah had a big heart, but how would she react now after seeing Shantel in action?

"She'll probably be back tomorrow. I'll put him to bed."

Will crossed the room and lifted Jordan from her arms. She stood and handed Will Jordan's jacket and backpack. Will fell into the familiar routine of preparing Jordan for bed and in minutes, Jordan lay curled up under the sheets. He planted a kiss on his forehead.

When he returned downstairs, Savannah stood by the door with her coat and shoes on. "It's getting late."

"Sorry about tonight." He glanced back at the stairs.

"No need to apologize. I understand." Savannah stepped closer and planted a kiss on his cheek. "Everything is going to work out."

Will pulled her into his arms and pressed his forehead against hers. "How can you be so sure?"

"Because of love."

Will took a deep breath and let her go. "Call me when you get home."

Savannah smiled at him. "Yes, sir."

Why did life have to be so complicated? No, why does my life have to be so complicated? Will thought as he watched Savannah pull away from the house. In a normal world, he would let himself fall for Savannah, even consider marriage. Instead, life pushed him around like a bully. The transfer, the shooting, Jordan, Savannah. As soon as he got comfortable in one place, life shoved hard and sent him reeling. When was he going to find stable ground?

Chapter 18

Will awoke, the previous evening swirling in his head. How did one night hold such contradictions? One second, he's kissing Savannah and the next minute he's putting Jordan to bed. He swung his legs out of bed, pressing his feet to the floor. After a few seconds, his thoughts began to stabilize, the coolness of the hardwood floors grounding him.

A squeal rang out from behind him and before he could turn, Jordan dived into the bed. His grin threatened to outshine the sunlight streaming through the windows. "Good morning!"

Will turned to look at him. This was a huge improvement from last night. Jordan's heartbreak was so heavy Will had thought the boy was going to drown in it. "Good morning."

"What's for breakfast?"

Will laughed. "Whatever you make."

Jordan's face contorted like he was in deep thought. "Peanut butter, celery and raisins."

Will made a gagging sound. "Never mind. I'll make breakfast." He swatted at Jordan. "You need to get ready for school."

Jordan rolled over, his little fist clutching a handful of sheet. "Noooo."

"No arguing. Let's go."

Jordan let out a huff and climbed out of the bed with a fake scowl. "Okay."

"Do you have a clean uniform in your room?"

Jordan paused. "Mom made me put one in my backpack."

Will looked down at his feet to avoid Jordan seeing his frown. She had this all planned out. "Just one?"

"Yes." That probably meant she would be back to get him today.

"All right, go get ready." He exhaled as Jordan's footfalls slapped down the hallway. He would have to talk to the boy about last night even though he wasn't sure what he would say. Shantel said he could have Jordan. Oh, how he wished that was true.

Will showered and dressed, and then headed down to start breakfast. Bacon, eggs and toast would have to do. When he opened the fridge, he spotted the pie Savannah had brought. An evening cut short. Maybe he could invite her back over once Jordan left, if the pie lasted that long.

"Are we going to Nana's house for dinner tonight?" Jordan climbed up into one of the bar stools at the counter. Will smiled at him. "That depends on what your mother does, but I'll see what I can do."

"I miss Nana."

"I'm sure Nana misses you, too."

Will scrambled the eggs while the bacon crackled in another pan.

"So is Miss Savannah your girlfriend?"

Will groaned. Nothing like getting interrogated about your love life by a six year old. "Sorta."

Jordan grinned. "I like her. She's hot."

Will shot him a narrowed eyed gaze as he drained the bacon on a paper towel. "What do you know about that?"

Jordan giggled. "Okay. She's pretty."

Will dished some eggs and bacon on a plate and sat it in front of Jordan. "I'm glad you approve."

"If you marry her, we can be a real family."

Will paused. "Jordan."

Jordan gaped at him. "She's nice. She would be a good mommy. She let me fall asleep in her lap last night. She smells good."

"You have a mommy." Will served himself. Not the way he wanted to breech this subject, but it was out there now.

Jordan looked down at his food. "She…she's not a very good one."

Will rubbed Jordan's head. "Your mom is going through a rough time right now. I'm sure she'll be a good mommy once she's better."

Jordan looked up at him with wide eyes. "How is she going to get better when she's drunk all the time?"

"What?"

"Mom drinks. Half of the time she doesn't answer her phone because she's sleep from drinking. Derrick drinks, too."

Will's stomach turned, his food no longer appetizing. If Shantel was a good mom, why on earth would she be drunk around her son? "Bless the food, Jordan and pray for your mommy."

As Jordan said the shortest prayer in history, Will prayed, too. *Lord, if there is any way I can keep Jordan like Shantel said, please…*He left the prayer unfinished.

After breakfast, Jordan packed his backpack while Will fixed him a lunch. Jordan maintained a happy chatter as they left the house and the entire car ride to the school. The sidewalk outside Jordan's school reminded Will of salmon swimming upstream. Children squealed and jostled with their friends. Others strained against the grip of their parents. Not Jordan. He wore the widest grin.

Shantel didn't call the night before. Will had called a couple of times, but if Jordan's revelation at breakfast was true, she was probably sleeping off her hangover. As much as Will enjoyed the feel of Jordan's hand in his, something would have to give. Shantel would have to pull herself together before his transfer. She would have no one to run to her rescue.

Will signed into the school's visitor log in the office and walked Jordan to his classroom.

Ms. Jackson's eyebrows rose when she spotted Will at the door. "Mr. Anderson."

Will nodded and eased Jordan in the door. "Good morning, Ms. Jackson. Can I speak to you for a moment."

Jordan grinned. "Bye, Dad."

Will hugged the boy. "Have a good day."

Ms. Jackson stepped into the hallway. "Good to see you."

"I need to ask a favor. If Jordan's mother doesn't come to pick him up, could you please call me?"

Ms. Jackson frowned. "I thought you wanted me not to call anymore."

Will rubbed his face and tried not to choke on his own words. "I know, but his mother has some issues going on right now."

"She's had some issues for a while. I've been very concerned about Jordan since he had that accident on the playground." She sighed. "If it wasn't for you, I would have called child welfare. Then I learned you were transferring."

Will swallowed. "Thank you for taking care of Jordan. I promise I will try to make things better before I leave."

She glanced in the classroom at Jordan. "I hope so for Jordan's sake."

The sunshine outside burned too brightly in his eyes. If Ms. Jackson had called child welfare, he would have lost Jordan forever. He needed to talk to Shantel and Derrick. Jordan could not go into the foster care system.

*

Carrie walked into Savannah's office holding an armful of mail. She sat it on the corner of Savannah's desk. "I have good news and bad news."

Savannah's mind drifted to Jordan's tears the night before. "Good news first."

"We are officially sold out of tickets."

Savannah clapped her hands, fighting back tears. "Finally something going right." She eyed Carrie. "What's the bad news?"

"Your ex-fiancé bought a ticket this morning."

Savannah groaned. "Why can't he leave me alone?"

Carrie snapped her fingers. "I got it. I think you should tell Will about him. I'm sure there's some legal form of intimidation he can use to scare Mitch off."

Savannah huffed. "Mitch doesn't have much love or fear for the FBI."

"I still think you should try."

Carrie's words lingered long after she'd gone. What would Will think about Mitch? She wouldn't even know what to tell him. How would she word her suspicions? Mitch hadn't done anything specific to make her believe that he was trying to hurt her now. Will probably wouldn't appreciate chasing down another dead end.

Savannah reached for the mail, determined to sort it before the end of the day. A large manila envelope lay at the bottom of the pile. The return address was from Georgia. Probably the information from Daddy.

She held the envelope in her hand a few seconds longer. Her father would hold her to her promise, but for the time being, she had enough on her plate. She would get to it as soon as things calmed down from the gala. Daddy wouldn't be happy, but she would remind him that she had an organization to run and side projects would have to take a back seat.

*

Will sat with his head cradled in his hands, his emotions swirling and threatening to erupt. It seemed his thoughts were stretched taunt and to the point of breaking. His shooters were dead. So was Juan Valdez. Neither shooting provided Will with any new information. He wasn't sure if Shantel was going to pick Jordan up from school or not. Then there was Savannah. He wanted to talk to her but not in this state. He would probably end up telling her that he loved her.

He lifted his head. He loved Savannah. Too bad that wasn't his problem. It was what to do about that love. He remembered the first day he'd seen her in her sunny yellow suit. Somehow, that was the association his mind clung to. Sunshine. She brightened a place that he long left dark.

He stared at all the info on the case spread out on his extremely messy desk. Something had to make sense. There had to be closure somewhere in this. Dead ends or not, someone was still responsible for trafficking both sets of women in the case. If it was Pablo, then Will needed to make sure the operation didn't continue despite the loss of its leader. There were still some live leads on this case. They only needed more time to be explored.

His desk phone rang. "Agent Anderson."

"Hey, Will. It's Zach. You busy?"

Will glanced around his office. "Not really. Just trying to make sense of all this evidence on this case."

"I may be able to help. I got some info to find your guy."

Will sighed. "I already found him."

"That's great."

"I found him dead."

"Oh, man. That's bad."

"Yeah."

"Well, this may be a day late and a dollar short, but it may give you some answers." Will heard papers shuffling. "I researched using the parameters you gave me and came up with a case you worked right after you joined."

Will sat forward. "Did it involve an angry family member?"

"Angry is putting it mild," Zach continued. "This dude, Pablo Varon, threatened to cause trouble for everyone involved in the case of his little brother, Juan Varon."

So he was using his little brother's name as an alias. "What was his beef with me?"

"You apparently singlehandedly brought down a trafficking ring out at the piers at Dundalk. You don't remember that?" Zach laughed. "The report said you were doing patrols and spotted something odd near the pier. When you went to investigate, the suspects fled and you chased this guy Juan for almost five blocks before you caught him."

"Yeah, I do remember. I cuffed the guy to a gate, called for backup and went back and found—" Will shook his head, the memory sharpening. "I found drugs, guns and three underage girls in a cargo crate."

"That's right. That wasn't the whole story. Juan got convicted, but not before flipping on some of his associates in the drug cartel. He was killed in prison."

Will rubbed his face. "That explains Pablo's hatred toward me." As illogical as it was, Pablo probably held Will responsible for his brother's death.

"If Pablo wasn't dead, I would have told you to take a closer look at him. This guy has a string of near-misses with the law."

"Explain near-misses."

"He's been arrested dozens of times, but nothing ever stuck. For instance, he was suspected of human trafficking in Georgia. That case went the furthest of all the others, to an indictment, but then all the charges abruptly dropped."

A wave of alertness washed over Will. Georgia. Savannah's home state. Maybe that was the missing piece on how Savannah was involved. If this guy was in Georgia… "Thanks Zach, this was helpful."

"Good. Don't forget, we need to get together before you take off to California."

Right, the transfer. It had been several days since Will had even thought about it. "I'll get in touch."

Will hung up and immediately logged into the NCIC database. He typed in Pablo's name and to his surprise, pages of cases popped up. *Probably not all the same guy.* He narrowed his search to those including trafficking of anything and to those in Georgia. That gave him 10 cases, three of which were conducted by the FBI in Georgia. Maybe they'd uncovered enough about how the trafficking ring worked to give Will some insight about what Pablo could have done in DC.

A rush of excitement coursed through his veins as he dialed the number for the investigator on one of the cases, an Agent Patterson. The phone rang and rang, and then went to voicemail. Will nearly let out a growl but stifled it. "Agent Patterson, my name is Agent Will Anderson and I have some questions about a case you worked. A Pablo Varon." He rattled off the case numbers. "Seems that Pablo may have moved his organization up here. Please give me or Officer Grant at MPD a call." Will stated both he and Grant's phone numbers. He ended the call feeling more hope than he had in days.

He turned back to his computer and continued his search. Within a half an hour, he knew considerably more about Pablo Varon. He had most of Pablo's previous addresses and his visa information which confirmed Marisol's assertion that she'd met the man in Guatemala. Not hard since Pablo was Guatemalan. Will's anger churned at the fact that this man had no national pride, trafficking his fellow countrywomen.

Will's cell phone rang, buzzing him out of his search. "Hello."

"Mr. Anderson, this is Ms. Jackson. You asked me to call you if Miss Richardson didn't pick up Jordan."

"I'll be right there."

As Will filed his notes and shut down his computer, his heart grew heavier and heavier. Jordan didn't deserve this. He trotted down to Carter's office, but found it empty. He jotted off a note explaining what he'd found and where he'd gone and stuck it to Carter's monitor. *Thank goodness for this transfer because I wouldn't be as flexible.* The thought materialized and Will rebuked himself. No, this transfer wasn't good. It only made his life more challenging. So much for a clean break despite his attempts to keep things from getting messy.

He retrieved his phone and dialed Savannah's number to invite her to dinner with he and Jordan. He may as well enjoy the mess.

Chapter 19

A stiff wind greeted Will and Jordan as they left for school after another night together. After another night of no Shantel. The coolness of the breeze only added to the chill Will felt. He wished he could have a little more time with Jordan. They'd had a great dinner with Savannah, who seemed to take his unusual parental arrangement in stride. Will had marveled at her ability to connect with Jordan. Then again, that was her specialty: connecting with people. They'd chatted like old friends all night about everything from school to Savannah's gala. Will had sat back and watched their interactions with a heart full of love for both of them.

Will stopped in front of the school and turned on his hazard lights. "All set?"

Jordan nodded.

Will rubbed the boy's head. "Have a good day."

"Okay, Dad."

Jordan opened the door.

"Wait." Will reached for Jordan. "If your mother doesn't show up, have Ms. Jackson call me again." He would have to work out childcare if she didn't since he would be attending the gala with his mother, his normal backup babysitter.

Jordan's face fell. "I don't want to go with her. She doesn't want me. Why can't I just stay with you?"

Will sighed. "Jordan, this is all difficult, but it will get better. I promise. You believe me?"

Jordan clutched his bag and pouted. "Yes."

Will kissed Jordan on the forehead. "Now get."

Jordan giggled and hopped out of the car.

Will watched Jordan disappear inside before he pulled off, secretly hoping Shantel didn't pick Jordan up again. It was hard to admit that his mother was right, but he enjoyed every minute he spent with Jordan. For the second time that week, he reconsidered his transfer.

The first had come during Savannah's visit for dinner. She and Jordan had hit it off so well. They'd spent a cozy evening together which left Will longing for more like it. Could he cancel his transfer and stay? Shantel's now frequent disappearances added to his musings. What would Jordan do if Will wasn't there? Shantel's family could barely care for themselves. They had never once offered to help despite the fact that they lived in the same city. Sending Jordan to them would be as bad as him staying with Shantel.

Will parked in the garage and by the time he made it to the office, the decision to talk to Carter about his transfer had been made. When he stepped inside, he was taken aback by the buzz. Several agents, to his surprise, greeted him when he passed. *What on earth is going on?* He walked to his desk. Papers half covered it. Not the look of a transferring agent.

"You've been busy. You've got some new developments on your case?"

Will jolted. Agent Carter stood at the door of his cubicle. "Yeah. Alexandria PD found the man from the sketch dead in a motel on Route 1."

"I heard. It seems this case is bigger than we first expected. Looks like you uncovered a major trafficking ring." Carter leaned against the gray felted wall. "Alexandria and Montgomery county PD called for you yesterday. They saw your BOLO bulletin for the white box truck and the sketch of your man."

Will frowned. "But we found him."

"The calls were about the truck. Seems like a lot of people have seen your guy driving his truck around the area. Both of those departments did a little investigating and found four more brothels."

Will's jaw dropped. "You're kidding."

"Nope. Thirty more girls. They're being processed by different agencies but they seem like they'd just got here."

Will sank into his chair. "Do we have anymore useful information, like who is running this ring?"

Carter shook his head. "Everything points to your suspect."

Will shook his head. "I don't think so. If he was in charge, he wouldn't be doing all the grunt work."

"That's true. With all the info we have, it's bound to lead us to more suspects."

Will looked at the papers on his desk. "That's what I'm hoping."

Carter straightened. "Well, I have total faith in you. If anyone is going to close this case, it's you. I hate to see you go."

Will grimaced. "About that. I was wondering if we could talk."

"Let's step into my office."

Will rubbed his clammy palms against his pants and walked into Carter's office. *Okay, God. I promised my mother I'd pray. I need some confirmation that I'm doing the right thing.*

Carter closed the door behind him. "What's up?"

"How hard would it be to cancel my transfer?"

Carter stopped, gaping at Will with surprise, and then he sat in his chair. "You're pretty far into the process."

"I know, but I don't think it's good for me to leave now."

"Is this about your son?"

Will sighed. "You know he's not really my son—"

Carter held up a hand to stop him. "Legally, maybe not. As far as I'm concerned, he is."

Will looked down at his hands. "It seems his mother is having a hard time with him and his biological father isn't around much."

"I always believed you might have a case against her. At least visitation rights." Carter crossed his arms. "If you stay, I know a good lawyer that may be able to help you."

Will smiled. "Thanks, sir."

Carter picked up his phone. "So should I call the California office?"

Will rose. "Not yet. Let me talk this over with my family first." *And Savannah.*

Carter returned the receiver to the base and nodded. "When you're ready."

"Thank you, sir."

"You're more than welcome. Now go solve your case."

Chapter 20

Both pressure and relief grew in Savannah's heart. The gala was tonight, which brought on the relief. This was almost over. Her life could get back to some form of normal after this. The pressure arose from all the details she had to manage between now and tonight.

She checked off another one of those details as she walked out of the ballroom where the gala would be held at the Gaylord National Harbor. Thank goodness for the event planning company she'd hired. She smiled at all they'd done to the room. They had suggested simple elegance, since fundraising for human trafficking wasn't exactly a cheerful topic. Although, she needed all the cheer she could get.

Her dinner with Will and Jordan two days ago had lifted her spirits quite a bit, more than she expected. She thought it would have been tense after the scene with Jordan's mother. However, within five minutes of being in the room with Will and Jordan, she realized that Shantel was the source of stress for the two. The two boys seemed to get along wonderfully and Will proved to be the great dad she expected him to be.

251

The sun sparkled off the waters of the Potomac as she drove away from the National Harbor and brought on a euphoric wandering in her mind. Thoughts of family. A family with Will and Jordan. She hadn't missed the little boy's hints about Savannah becoming a more permanent fixture in he and his father's life. Savannah had watched Will closely every time Jordan mentioned it. Will didn't look completely opposed to it, but he certainly couldn't do anything now. With the time before his transfer ticking away, what could he do?

How would Savannah respond if he did suggest something more? Did she want to be in a relationship with a man living on the other side of the country? To her surprise, she realized that she would if the man was Will. Besides, Will wouldn't stay away for long. He would surely come up with a plan for them to be reunited and she would happily wait.

The office was empty when she returned to Plateau. Carrie had as many tasks as Savannah to complete. She deserved a couple of days off once all this is done. She earned it. The quiet seeped into her bones as she entered her office. Definitely the quiet before the storm.

Savannah straightened her desk to leave. She spied the manila envelope from her father sitting on the edge of her desk. Might as well give it a quick glance just in case her father asked her about it tonight. It would have to be a quick look. She still needed to go home and get dressed. She ripped opened the folder and pulled out the papers inside.

On top of the pile was a handwritten note from Carl Hughes, the Georgia state's attorney expressing his hope of her being a great help with the investigation. Under that, a police report. Savannah read through it and picked up the important points. The Arizona police had a man in custody that gave them the location of the grave. Savannah read the man's name, but didn't recognize it. She would have to look through the files to see if the name was connected to any other trafficking victims she'd helped. Trafficking networks could be vast, easily encompassing the east and west coast. *If I only had a picture of the suspect.*

Savannah placed the police report to the side, making a mental note to request a mug shots of the suspects. Then she noticed the photos. They displayed a few angles at the mass grave. She studied each one, which had more FBI officers in it than anything else. She flipped to the last picture in the file and gasped. It showed a container sitting in the dirt. Savannah pressed her hand to her lips. *That container.*

She barely made it to the trashcan beside her desk before she retched up what little she had in her stomach. Tears filled her eyes and she pressed them closed. Images from that night in the warehouse appeared. The coolness of the room, despite the hot Georgia weather. The men on the far side of the warehouse floor were unceremoniously putting people into body bags. No, corpses. On the left side, four men were loading the newly filled body bags into huge brown crates. Container marked with a strange logo.

Even though that night had happened a year ago, the terror returned as strong as it had been that night, trapping Savannah between the night that changed her life and the present. She vomited again, the sting of stomach acid coating her throat. *You stood there and watched and didn't say a word.* She let out a sob. Now those poor souls had been found, no thanks to her. She'd had several opportunities to provide more information to the FBI but fear had kept her silent. The same fear she'd seen in the countless victims she'd helped. Fear that if her secret were revealed, her life would be in danger.

She managed to sit up in her chair. She grabbed a tissue from her desk and wiped her mouth. Tossing it in the trash, she tied the trash bag closed. She lifted the bag and carried it out of the building to the dumpster. She bit back tears with each step.

As she tossed the bag and turned to go back inside, she caught sight of the parking lot. Like a flood, the memory of her near kidnapping flooded her mind. Her thoughts seemed sharper. The man who tried to kidnap her. He sounded familiar. So did the sketch Will had shown Marisol.

In a blink, the two snapped together in her thoughts. She clapped her hand to her mouth, stifling a yelp. The man in the sketch was the man who tried to kidnap her. She knew it was him even though she hadn't seen her kidnapper's face. She didn't need to. She'd seen him before…in Georgia.

The man in the sketch was head foreman in Mitch's warehouse. He was one of the men helping load the bodies into the containers that horrible night.

Knees wobbling, she ran back inside, but was still unable to escape her thoughts. If the man, Pablo if she remembered correctly, had trafficked Marisol into the US, there was a good chance that Mitch was still involved in human trafficking. Since the night at the warehouse, she'd wanted to believe it was a one-time event, but Marisol shattered that delusion. She could have stopped him. She'd kept her mouth shut, which means that she was partially responsible for Marisol's condition.

She ran to her office. Panting, she looked around, her eyes drifting to the papers on her desk. Her stomach turned again. *You need to tell someone.* She squeezed her eyes shut, tears trickling out. Yes, she did. She'd used her shame as an excuse long enough. Who knew how many women Pablo had managed to bring into the country the past year?

No more hiding. She rushed to her desk and grabbed her cell phone. She needed to talk to Will first. As she dialed, shame reared its head again. She wasn't ready to face Will, not yet. That, however, didn't absolve her from letting someone know. She changed direction and used her computer to pull up the number for the FBI's anonymous tip line.

She dialed the first three numbers before she heard a loud rap on the door outside. Before she could end her call, she heard the front door open. "Savannah?"

Her veins iced. *Mitch.* How did…

"Savannah, I know you're here. I saw you come in."

She dropped the phone on the base and looked around for somewhere to hide. Finding nothing, she considered escaping to one of the other offices and hiding there, but Mitch appeared at the door before she could move from her chair.

"Hello, Ladybug. Shouldn't you be gone for the evening?"

She tried to look calm, and then noticed the photos lying on her desk. She swept them up in one motion and shoved them back into the envelope. "What are you doing here?"

He leaned on the doorframe. "I was coming to see if you had everything under control for tonight."

She put on mock anger to hide her terror. "I don't need your help."

"Oh, yes you do." He moved closer to her desk. "More than you know."

She stepped back, bumping her legs against the chair.

He held up his hands. "I'm not going to hurt you. Why would I, especially since you've proven your loyalty ten times over."

"My loyalty?"

Mitch smiled. "I wanted to tell you that you're safe. I took care of the guy bothering you. You won't have to worry about him anymore."

Savannah gripped the edge of the desk to keep herself upright. "I don't know what you're talking about."

Mitch tipped his head. "Oh, yes you do. I can't have my employees acting without my approval."

Savannah dropped her head, and noticed that the contact page for the FBI was still on her screen. Her heart pounded. "I want you to leave."

In one fluid movement, Mitch moved around the desk. His eyes immediately went to her monitor. He reached over to her mouse and clicked to exit the screen. "You don't want to do that."

Savannah's heart faltered. "What you did was wrong, Mitch. Those poor girls…"

Mitch waved his hand. "You want to keep quiet. I would hate for something bad to happen to you." He gripped her chin, squeezing. "Something really bad especially now. It's such a big night for you."

She yelped and he released her. She stumbled away from him. "Are you going to kill me?"

He exaggerated the shake of his head. "If I find out that you talked to anyone, including Agent Will Anderson, I'll implicate you in my business. You did, after all, keep quiet about criminal activity for over a year. Won't be hard to convince law enforcement that you were involved."

Shock rocked Savannah backwards. "You know I didn't have anything to do with that."

"I know." He shrugged. "I don't want to do it, but if you call anyone, you'll leave me no choice." He gripped her arm. "You should be going."

She snatched away and a sardonic laugh erupted from her, surprising herself and Mitch. "Unless you're going to follow me everywhere I go, which tonight would be slightly impossible, you can't stop me from calling law enforcement."

Mitch stared at her, and then a slow grin bloomed on his face. "Nice try, Ladybug. I haven't run a successful business for years without having some help from law enforcement." He lifted his hands and studied his nails. "It's amazing how you can buy people for so many purposes here in America. Now you should get going."

Mitch stayed with her until she left the building and walked to her car. Savannah kept quiet but her thoughts were ablaze. *Threaten me all you want, Mitch, but I know one member of law enforcement that you can't buy.* She didn't need to call the FBI. The FBI was coming to her.

Chapter 21

Every five minutes, Savannah glanced around the room, her gaze stopping at the door. Where was Will? She fought to control her worry. It was early still. He would be here, and then she would tell him everything.

Well-dressed guests repeatedly stopped her to tell her how much they admired her work. Each time, when guilt should have slammed her, she felt peace. Peace that she was doing the right thing at last.

She made her rounds through the room as Josh and Dawn arrived. They both wore bright smiles.

Dawn rushed to her and gave her a hearty hug. "Oh, Savannah. This is so incredible."

Josh waited for his turn and then embraced Savannah. "It is. I'm so proud of you, baby sis."

Savannah fought back tears. Their support had always bolstered her courage. She needed that tonight more than ever. "Thank you. I'm so happy you're here."

They talked a little longer about the evening and Savannah fought to keep her attention on the conversation. She scanned the room. *I should keep an eye out for Mitch, too.* He wouldn't be so crazy to try something in such a public setting, but she wouldn't put anything past him. Another guest greeted her, and as she turned, she spotted a welcome sight.

Will.

He helped his mother with her coat, dressed in a gray tux. Her heart thundered. Her feet longed to run to him and throw herself in his arms.

Both Josh and Dawn turned in the direction of Savannah's gaze. Dawn's mouth formed an O. "My, he is handsome."

Yes, he is.

Josh feigned injury. "I'm going to take my wife and find our seats."

Dawn clutched his arm. "You know I didn't mean he's more handsome than you."

"Unh huh." Josh led her away.

Savannah watched them go, still smiling.

"You must be thinking about something wonderful." Mitch voice sent her stomach dropping to her toes. It was like he had materialized like a phantom.

She turned to face him and tried to keep smiling. "Just thinking about something I need to do."

Mitch nodded. "Anything I can help you with?"

Before Savannah could open her mouth, her parents appeared.

"There you are, honey." Daddy grinned at her and Savannah gave him a quick hug.

Esther leaned over and gave her a peck on the cheek. "You look beautiful tonight."

She accepted her mother's compliment, playing into the show that she and Esther put on whenever they were at public functions. "I thought you didn't like me in pink," Savannah said, sending a quick glance across the room. She nearly groaned. Where had Will gone?

Mitch grinned. "I think she looks lovely."

Savannah's stomach churned. "Thank you."

Her father rubbed his hands together. "Did you get the package from the state's attorney?"

Savannah kept her smile firmly in place. "Yes."

Mitch glared at her.

"Is this about whatever you're helping him with? Can we not talk business for one night?" Esther patted James' arm.

"Only a little business talk, Esther. Besides, the sooner we can identify those poor people the better."

Mitch put on a thoughtful look. "Is this about the mass grave? What a sad situation."

Savannah faced him. "Very sad. What kind of monster would do such a thing?" She looked at him pointedly. "What do you think?"

Esther let out a short laugh. "Savannah, what would Mitch know about such things?"

More than you know.

Mitch eyed her as her father changed the subject to politics. She needed to find Will and tell him about Mitch as soon as possible. She had been silent too long.

*

Will led his mother into the ballroom. He fought the urge to drag her along. All day, Savannah hadn't left his thoughts. He wanted to ask her about Pablo, yes, but more than that, he wanted to see her. He tried to imagine what she would wear tonight. Whatever it was, he was sure she would look stunning.

He had also worried that he wouldn't see her tonight if Shantel didn't pick Jordan up. He'd waited by his phone until 5 pm, well after the time the school offices closed, before he pulled his tux from the closet. Jordan wouldn't be happy about going home with Shantel and Will already had a plan to visit him tomorrow. He would demand to see the boy, especially since he knew that Shantel and Derrick were borderline absentee parents.

He would tell them both about the possibility of him staying in DC. He expected that their reactions would be very different from his mother's, who screamed for joy when he told her on the car ride over. After them, he only had one more person to tell. He prayed Savannah would react like his mother, too.

As Will helped his mother with her coat, he narrowed his eyes and searched the room. He nearly dropped the coat when he saw Savannah. She looked lovelier than he could imagine in a mauve dress that highlighted her shape and her hair pinned up in an elegant bun. His heart thudded. *Please let her be excited about me staying.*

The closely placed tables made it a little challenging for Will to navigate across the room to Savannah. Even though a cluster of people huddled around her, she stood like a siren, just at the side of the dance floor. Will's heart hitched. Her beauty eclipsed everything around her. When she noticed him and his mother approaching, she beamed. Mitch, who stood at her side, scowled.

"Hi, Will." She stepped to him, cupped his face and planted a warm kiss on his lips that lingered long enough to send heat all the way down to his toes.

Whoa. When did their relationship progress to public affection?

He swallowed his surprise. "Hi, there."

She linked her arm in his the same way she'd done at the restaurant.

Was something wrong? His brain had fogged over from the kiss.

"Daddy, I want you to meet Agent Will Anderson. Will, this is my father, Governor James Elliott." She pulled him to face the man next to her mother.

"Nice to meet you." Will shook the man's hand, noting the air of confidence that only a politician could exude.

"Nice to finally see the man who saved my daughter." James pumped Will's hand vigorously. "I am forever in your debt."

From his peripheral vision, Will saw Mitch's expression grow more sour than before.

Savannah's mother stepped to him and extended her hand. "Good to see you again, Will."

Will bit back a grin. Esther's face told him otherwise. She probably had plans to have Savannah spend the event at Mitch's side and it was clear Savannah wasn't leaving Will's.

Savannah motioned toward his mother. "This is Will's mother, Denise Anderson, the civil rights activist."

"What an honor." James grasped both Denise's hands.

Denise smiled. "Thank you."

A strange moment of quiet descended on the group and the music from the band started.

"Will, let's dance."

This time Will didn't catch his surprise in time. "Now?"

"This will probably be the only time I get to tonight." Savannah tugged at his arm.

Maybe she needed to get away from Mitch and her parents. "All right." He glanced around the circle. "If you'll excuse us." He turned Savannah toward to dance floor, but not before seeing the scowl on Mitch's face.

Will led her out to the middle of the empty dance floor. He pulled her into his arms and she placed a hand on his shoulder. "As much as I enjoyed that kiss, I realize it wasn't for my benefit. What's going on?"

Savannah ran her hand along the back and then tipping his head forward until her lips were at his earlobe. His heart hammered as he eyed the soft line of her neck. He'd only have to move in a few inches more to nuzzle it.

Focus. He squeezed his eyes tight and turned his head away from her neck.

"I need to talk to you about something important. I think I have some evidence concerning your case," she whispered.

Will stiffened. "What evidence?"

"I should have said something sooner, but I was too afraid."

"You're telling me now and that's a good thing."

Savannah took a deep breath. "I know the man in the sketch. Pablo."

Did she remember that Pablo was dead? Will held his tongue.

"He used to work for Mitch's company, King Sugar."

The revelation hit him like a cold blast of air. If he worked for Mitch then that meant...

"How do you know that?" He glanced over her shoulder at Mitch. He still stood in the same spot, alone, anger twisting his features.

"I saw him in Mitch's warehouse last year."

Will pulled back and looked in her eyes. The fear he saw there rattled him.

"Are you sure?"

She nodded and then sank back into his arms, pressing her cheek against his chest. "Mitch and I had just gotten engaged. I'd gone to his warehouse's office one night to discuss invitations with him. He wasn't there so I put some samples on his desk." She took a deep breath. "As I left, I noticed activity on the warehouse floor." Her voice faltered. Will pulled her closer, hoping to steady her while she finished her tale.

"I went down to see if he was there. When I got there-" she took a deep breath, her tiny ribcage expanding against his hold. "When I got there Mitch and his men were loading body bags into a crate."

Shock numbed his legs. Will reminded himself to keep dancing. "Did they see you?"

"I don't think so. Mitch must have figured out that I was there. I'd left the invitations on his desk but he never said anything about it."

"You never told anyone?"

Savannah shook her head. "No. I almost told my brother the night it happened but didn't."

Another song began. "Mitch's involvement may be hard to prove."

Savannah peered up at him. "Would pictures help?"

Will frowned. "You have pictures of them loading the bodies?"

"No but they buried the crate and the bodies in a rural area in Georgia. The police just found it a few weeks ago. They suspected that they were possible victims of human trafficking." Savannah stole a glance over her shoulder. "My father asked me to help out. He sent me pictures of the container and I recognized it from Mitch's warehouse."

Will sighed. "I'll have to confirm your story, but would you be willing to testify?"

Savannah looked up at him, sadness pooling in her eyes. "Yes. I want to make this right."

Mitch was the big fish. Could this get more complicated?

*

Who knew that finally bringing her secret to light would feel so freeing? The fear that had encased her heart for so long melted away in a moment. Being in Will's arms helped. He would make sure the people in that crate got justice. He made another turn along with the rhythm, his breath tickling her shoulder. She didn't want to leave his embrace.

The squeal of a microphone filled the air and the music stopped. *What in the world?*

Savannah spun around to see her father on the stage.

"What is he doing?" Will glanced over at her with a frown. "I take it this wasn't on the schedule of events."

"No."

Once he'd gotten everyone's attention, James raised the microphone to his lips. "Good evening, everyone and welcome. So glad to see you all tonight."

Anger stewed in her stomach as Savannah pulled away from Will and headed toward the stage. "Excuse me," she said and Will followed her from the dance floor.

She didn't get far before her mother intercepted her. "Where are you going?" Esther asked, grabbing Savannah's arm.

Savannah pulled her arm away. "To see why my father is on stage at my fundraiser."

Mama grabbed her arm again. "He only wants to say a few words."

This time Savannah yanked her arm away. "Then he should have asked me first."

Mama backed down. She would never let on that their happy family wasn't as happy as it looked to the casual observer.

"I want to thank you all for coming to my daughter's event. She's worked so hard to help so many and your support will help her do so much more."

Savannah held in the groan on her lips. *Why don't you just embarrass me in front of a room full of people?*

Josh appeared at her side. "What is going on? I didn't know he was on the program."

Savannah gave him a dry look. "He wasn't."

Daddy droned on. "Plateau is committed to helping victims all over the world. As a matter of fact, the organization is working with me as a consultant on the recent mass grave found in my state."

Savannah stopped in her tracks. She whipped around and spotted Will standing next to her mother, wearing a perplexed look. Standing five feet away from them, Mitch gave her a cold stare, his eyes narrowing.

God help me.

"Savannah and her crew are committed to ending human trafficking in the world and so am I." Daddy clasped his hands together. "That's why I have decided to run for the Senate."

Although people around her applauded, she stood frozen, her mind refusing what she'd just heard. How could he use her event, an event to help victims and bring awareness to their suffering and the heinous crimes committed against then, to announce his run for Senate?

"Please be generous tonight to help the victims of human trafficking. It will greatly be appreciated."

Savannah reached the edge of the stage just as he placed the microphone back on its stand. He glided down the stairs and gave her a bright smile. "Hi, princess."

"How dare you?" She didn't bother lowering her voice. Several guests at the tables nearby paused and looked at them.

His smile faltered a little. "I'm not sure what you're talking about, Sweetheart."

Savannah put her hands on her hips. "No amount of pet names is going to change the fact that you're wrong and you know you're wrong."

He put on his *I'm-clueless* face. "I only wanted to greet everyone."

Savannah stepped closer. "This is my event and if you wanted to greet everyone, you should have run it by me first. Clearly, you wanted to tell everyone about your senate run. I'm not stumping for you anymore, Daddy. This is my event."

Esther slid up beside them. "I think you two need to take this conversation outside. It's bad form."

Savannah whipped around to her. "You would know about bad form. You'd think you'd get the message that I don't love Mitch anymore but you keep throwing him at me like cold grits."

Mama's face paled. "You cannot speak to me like that. I'm only trying to help you see that you're passing up a good man."

Savannah opened her mouth to tell them what kind of man Mitch was, that he was up to his eyeballs in the very industry she'd spent the past year trying to combat and had probably murdered those people in the crate. Instead she snapped her mouth shut and turned to walk away.

"You can't keep running away from him now that he's a part of your father's campaign team." Mama's words washed over like an icy tidal wave.

She pivoted to face Daddy. "What?"

Daddy grinned. "Mitch is my campaign manager. He has already started the process of moving up here to help me once I get in office. Someone with his business sense is an asset."

Mitch working with her father. Her view narrowed, the lights brightened, and set her head pounding.

Josh's anger simmered to the surface. "How could you ask your daughter's ex-fiancé to be on your campaign team? You know they are not on good terms."

She pressed her hand to her forehead. "Oh, no. Daddy, he can't be."

"Savannah, what on earth has gotten into you?" Mama placed a hand on Savannah shoulder.

Savannah moved to her father. "You have to take him off your team. He's not who he appears to be."

James' face turned serious. "Did he hurt you, Baby?"

Esther glanced over Savannah's shoulder. "We can clear all of this up right now. Here comes Mitch."

Cold sweat prickled across her skin. Mitch stood about three tables away. She had to end this conversation.

"No, Mama. Please, you can't say anything."

Mama straightened her shoulders. "I can and I will. This is absolutely ridiculous. Mitch is a fine boy and I will not have you slander him."

Mitch glided up to her side. "Is everything all right?" he asked, sliding his arm around her waist like it belonged there.

Savannah spoke before her mother could, but at the same time stepped away from Mitch. "Everything's fine. Daddy's announcement caught me by surprise."

Mitch grinned. "So now you know the real reason I'm in DC."

Savannah looked into his eyes, her discomfort increasing. He was a man, a normal looking if not attractive man but he was a monster inside. No wonder he'd fooled Mama and Daddy because they never bothered to look any deeper than the surface. Had they peered a little deeper past their own ambitions, they would have seen the blackness of his heart. Or even stared into his eyes. Savannah could see it now, the cold disconnect. There had to be in order for him to commit such horrible crimes against others and hide behind stature and money.

She pulled away from Mitch. "I need to go." *I need to go find Will.*

"I'll keep my eye on you."

Savannah sucked in a breath. "Not necessary."

Mitch grasped her waist again. "If you have a moment, I'd like to talk to you."

Her throat tightened. She slipped out of his grasp and put Mama between him and her. "I need to get the program started."

She walked up to the stage, hands shaking. The sooner this night was over, the better.

Chapter 22

Just as Savannah took the stage, his phone rang. Scowling, he recognized the MPD extension. He rushed out into the hall, which was slightly quieter than the ballroom.

Will plugged one finger in his ear and pressed his phone to the other. "Hello?"

"Agent Anderson." Will barely made out Officer Grant's voice. "Did I catch you at a bad time?"

"Sort of." Will glanced over his shoulder at the door. Good thing this was his mother's kind of event and she didn't mind being left alone.

"Sorry," Grant said. "I'll keep this short then. Did you ask someone from Georgia FBI to call me?"

Will straightened. "Yes."

"Okay, they called me and gave me some information on our dead guy. Apparently, he was a suspect in a massive trafficking ring. Drugs, guns, people, you name it." Grant's voice grew louder. "He's been arrested quite a few times, but the agents in Georgia didn't believe that he was running it alone."

"Did they have any ideas on who was?" Will turned his back to the door, Savannah's words floating to his thoughts. "Is there any mention of King Sugar?"

There was a slight pause and then Officer Grant laughed. "Yeah. King Sugar is listed as Pablo's employer. You guys conducted an investigation on King Sugar just about a year ago. How did you know?"

"Can you call Georgia FBI back and tell them I have information that will help their case."

"Actually, I already told them to call you tonight. Your phone call stirred them up down there and they went over to King Sugar."

"And?"

"They found drugs and made some arrests. More interesting, one of the suspects gave them quite a good look into how the girls are getting to DC. As a matter of fact, there is a shipment of girls in DC or on their way. The FBI is searching trucks up and down I-95."

Will throat tightened. *Oh, God.* "Have they issued an arrest warrant for the owner, Mitchell Alverez?" *Please say yes.*

"No, but they do want to talk to him."

Will exhaled with a hiss. "He's here. I'll talk to him. Keep me posted."

"Will do. I'll keep working on this end."

Will slipped his phone back into his holster and pressed his fingertips to his forehead. It would have given him too much pleasure to arrest Mitch in front of Savannah, but he would have to settle for a good, long interview.

His phone buzzed. He whipped it out and answered without looking at the caller ID. "You got something new, Grant?"

"Will?" Shantel asked, a sniffle in her voice. "Will, are you there?"

"Shantel -" His mind ramped up but his stomach dropped. "Is Jordan okay?"

"I. . . " Her voice faded out. "Jordan is..."

"Say that again. I didn't hear you."

"I don't know where Jordan is. I think he ran away." Each of her words came through loud and clear, chilling him and numbing his fingers gripping the phone.

"He what?"

"We got into an argument. He got angry and told me that he would rather live with you. I sent him to his room, but I got distracted. I guess he left."

You guess? "Did your check with you neighbors?"

"He didn't go there."

Even over the sound of the noise inside, the slur in her words was blatant.

"Have you called the police?"

"Of course I have. They told me to call Jordan's father."

Will gritted his teeth. "You called me and not Derrick?"

"Derrick's in jail," she snapped.

Will ran his hand over his face. "I'm on my way."

"No! The police want you to go home in case Jordan shows up there."

"I'll be home in thirty minutes."

"Will, I'm sorry."

"We'll discuss this later." He ended the call, fear and anger churning in his chest. Shantel was drunk, Derrick was in jail and Jordan had run away.

He rushed back into the ballroom. "God, please protect my little boy."

*

As soon as Savannah stepped off the stage, Mitch was there.

He grinned. "Let's have that talk now." He grasped her arm. Anyone watching would have mistaken it for a light touch, but his grip was so tight that it threatened to bring tears to Savannah's eyes. He led her through the ballroom, even stopping numerous times for her to greet guests. Savannah's heart thumped with each of her footfalls. Mitch's grip dug into her arm as he hauled her toward the elevators.

I can't leave the building with him. Just as she geared herself up to scream, she saw Will coming toward her in long purposeful strides, a frown on his face. Mitch grip on her arm loosened. Her heart skittered.

Will stopped in front of her and Mitch's hand dropped away from her arm.

Free.

Will grasped her hand. "I need to talk to you." He glanced at Mitch. "I'm sorry, but this is urgent and I don't have much time."

Mitch nodded, and backed away. Will watched him go. Savannah could see the tension working in his jaw.

Savannah placed her hand over the spot where the heat of Mitch's handprint still lingered. "Is everything all right?"

Will shook his head. "Jordan ran away. I have to go home to see if he went there."

Savannah pressed her hand to his chest. "Oh, Will."

Will opened his mouth and then closed it. Anger simmered in his eyes. The desire to pull him into her arms nearly set her into motion, but Will's restless energy kept her from trying to still him for the embrace.

She squeezed his hand instead. "You need to go."

"Yeah." Will glanced over her shoulder. "I have to get my mother."

Savannah released his hand. "Right. If you need anything, please let me know."

Will nodded and stepped away.

Savannah glanced around. No Mitch. He must have slunk into a dark corner, or prayerfully left. Which would buy her some more time. Will's exit brought on feelings of more vulnerability. She would have to avoid Mitch. Not hard in a ballroom full of people.

*

Will gripped the steering wheel. Even with the police escort, he couldn't navigate his trip home fast enough. Topping seventy miles per hour in the residential areas, the streets of DC blurred past him as fast as his thoughts zipped through his mind. Jordan was a smart boy. He lived near one of the toughest areas in Southeast. He'd grasped Will's lessons on being street smart and most of the people in his neighborhood knew that Will worked for the FBI. No one would mess with Jordan.

Mom reached over and squeezed his knee. "He's probably sitting in front of your house."

Will nodded, not trusting himself to speak for fear that all his thoughts would tumble out. Mom sat in the seat quiet, probably battling her own fears. No, she was praying. That's what they needed.

"Mom, can you pray? Out loud?"

From his peripheral vision, he saw her gaze snapped to him. "Of course."

As Mom prayed, an odd peace filled the car and stilled his hammering heart. Her words were simple, but pierced Will's heart. Another pulse, hope, replacing his anxiety. Hope about Jordan, staying in DC and even hope that Savannah's tip would play out.

The police escort killed the sirens as they whipped into Will's driveway. Will threw the car in park and jumped from the car before it completely stopped. Mom met him at the front of the car.

The front step was empty.

Mom let out a strangled groaned.

Jordan didn't have a key and wouldn't have any way of getting inside, but Will and the police officer went through the house room by room, yelling Jordan's name. The search ended in the living room where Mom stood sniffling.

Will threw his arms around her, allowing her to cry tears for him. He couldn't allow the tide of emotion to overtake him yet. Jordan needed him to be clear-headed.

Once mom's tears tapered off, Will reached for his phone and dialed Shantel. She answered on the first ring.

"He's not here."

A sob filled his ear. "I told you to take him. If you had taken him, he would have been safe."

Will clenched his jaw and stepped away from his mother. "Shantel, now is not the time for this."

"You should have kept him!"

"When we find him, I will keep him." Will jabbed the button to end the call.

Mom gazed up at Will. "Do you mean that?"

Will exhaled. "Yes, mom. I'll fight to keep Jordan with my every breath."

She gave him a sad smile. "Let's continue to pray that Jordan comes home to us."

Chapter 23

Savannah eased into another cluster of guests and sent up another prayer for Jordan. He was far more innocent than she was, and God had rescued her from Mitch. Surely God would protect the boy.

Several people congratulated her on her father's run for Senate, probably assuming that she would benefit from his possible election. Maybe she would have if Mitch wasn't involved in the campaign. His conviction would be a black mark on her father's administration. From what she knew about Will, Mitch would be convicted.

One of the hostesses rushed up to her. "Miss Savannah. Carrie needs to see you at the front desk."

Savannah frowned and excused herself from her guests. "Did she say what she needed?"

The hostess shrugged. "She said something about a guest without a ticket."

The gala had already been going for almost two hours. Who could be arriving this late?

As she eased through the crowd, a red backpack near the elevator caught her eye. She frowned and focused on the backpack. Where had she seen that it before?

A guest, one of her daddy's friends, stepped out of her way to give her a full view of the front desk.

Jordan.

Despite her heels, Savannah broke into a run.

Jordan looked up at her, still dressed in his school uniform, and grinned. "Hi, Miss Savannah."

Hot tears filled her eyes. She scooped the boy up and kissed his forehead. "What are you doing here?"

He wiggled out of her grasp and giggled. "I came to see my dad. He told me he was going to be here."

"He left to look for you."

Jordan's face scrunched into a frown. "Oh."

Savannah grasped his hand. "Let's give him a call." Savannah ducked behind the ticket table, grabbed her purse that she had left hidden there, and fished her cell phone. She pulled Jordan behind the table, too.

Carrie smiled at Jordan. "How about I take you to get something to eat?"

Savannah tightened her grip on Jordan's hand. "How about you bring something to us?" She lowered her voice. "I don't want to let him out of my sight until his father gets here."

Carrie nodded.

With trembling fingers, Savannah dialed Will's number.

One ring. "Special Agent Anderson."

"Will, it's Savannah. Jordan is here."

"At the gala?"

"He came here looking for you."

"Does he look…okay? Is he hurt?"

"He looks fine. Why don't you talk to him?"

Jordan eyes widened as she handed him the phone. "Hi, Dad."

Carrie returned with a plate of hors de 'oeuvres. "I didn't know Will had a son."

Before Savannah could respond, Jordan stepped over to them and lifted the phone to her. "My dad wants to talk to you."

Savannah moved so that he could be closer to Carrie and the plate of food, but kept her hand on his shoulder. "Hello."

"Savannah, I cannot thank you enough for finding my son."

Savannah giggled. "He sort of found me."

"Either way, thank you. I know you're busy with your gala." He let out a ragged breath. "I'm on my way there with the police."

"Jordan won't leave my side until you get here."

"I love you." His voice sent warm ripples down her spine. So did his words. "What did you say?"

He cleared his throat. "I said I love you."

Savannah grinned. "I love you, too."

He let out a loud exhale and laughed. "I was hoping you'd say that."

*

Most of the gala guests had gone by the time Will and his mother rushed through the door.

No matter how much he'd tried to convince his mother to go home, she refused. His words to Shantel were wasted, too. She climbed out of a squad car that parked behind him.

Carrie waited at the front door. She eyed Shantel. "Jordan is back here."

Will wanted to run past Carrie as she led them into the main ballroom. Jordan stood next to Savannah. Will's heart soared. Those two looked good together.

Jordan spotted Will first. "Dad!" He bolted across the room and threw himself into Will's arms. Will held him tight, relishing his little boy smell. *Thank you, God.*

Will released him and his mother pulled Jordan into an embrace. Shantel stood back, biting her lip, tears in her eyes. Finally Jordan wiggled away from Denise and submitted to a limp hug from Shantel.

As soon as Shantel stepped back, Will stooped down to Jordan's eye level, scowling as much as he could. He would make sure Jordan understood what he'd done was dangerous, but his heart leapt with joy. "What are you doing here?"

Jordan's hands dropped to his side. "I came to see you." His voice rose to a squeak.

Will gripped his shoulders. "By yourself?

"Dad, I was safe. I called a cab."

Will bit his lip. "Okay. We'll talk about this later."

A police officer stepped over to Will. "Sir, we need to talk to your son and his mother."

Will stood. "Of course."

Jordan and Shantel followed the officer in silence. Will watched them go as Savannah approached. The soft smile on her lips stirred up his feeling for her. How could he even think that he could leave and live the rest of his life without her?

He didn't wait for her to reach him, closing the gap between them and pulled her into his arms. He cut off her words with a deep kiss. She yielded just as she had with their first kiss. She slid her arms around his shoulders.

He pulled away, breathless. "Thank you."

She blinked and her cheeks flushed to pink. "I didn't do anything."

"I'm not transferring."

She leaned back, surprise on her face. "What?"

"I talked to my boss a couple of days ago. I'm going to cancel my transfer and stay here and I was wondering if you—"

His words were cut off by Shantel, Jordan and the officer's return.

The officer tapped Will on the shoulder. "Can I speak with you, sir?"

"Of course." Will stepped away from Savannah, relishing the hope and happiness in her eyes. As soon as they got done with this Mitch business, they could start a life together.

Mitch. Will ground his teeth. He was supposed to question him tonight. As he and the officer stepped out of the room, he looked for Mitch, but didn't spot him.

Where did that weasel go?

The officer paused as soon as they were beyond the doors. "Sir, I understand that you have an interesting situation with the young man."

"Yes. I recently found out that I'm not his biological father."

The officer nodded. "I see." He sighed. "You didn't hear this from me, but I highly recommend you keep the young man with you tonight." The officer looked over his shoulder. "Let's just say that his mother is not in charge of all her faculties."

Will nodded. *That kills me talking to Mitch tonight and it may be harder to find him tomorrow.* "Right."

The officer departed and Will returned to the little cluster of people he'd left. "Okay, Jordan. We've had enough excitement for tonight. Time to go home."

Jordan looked up at Will, hope brimming in his eyes. "With you?"

His mother gave him a questioning glance.

Will turned to face Shantel. "With me."

Shantel pressed her lips together and dropped her head.

He leaned over and kissed Savannah on the cheek. "We'll talk more tomorrow about the information you gave me."

She sighed. "Yes."

Will grasped Jordan's hand and sighed, too. *Thank you, God for working this all out.*

Chapter 24

Savannah located the rest of her things, exhaustion weighing her every step. The night would have been draining even without the extra excitement. She was even too tired to really revel in Jordan's safe return and Will's announcement that he was staying. She would give it proper justice after many hours of sleep.

She would also have to save the extreme excitement about their fundraising efforts until tomorrow, but her heart sang. They'd raised almost five hundred thousand dollars between pledges and the ticket sales. She couldn't have wished for better. That would go a long way to helping victims, and she could do so with out the heavy guilt she'd bore for the past year.

The first thing on her to-do list tomorrow was to give a statement to Will. It probably wouldn't be too early since Will had Jordan for the night. She could be free from Mitch as soon as tomorrow night. That was worth celebrating, too.

She put on her coat and walked to the elevator. She looked for Carrie, but didn't see her. *Probably collecting her stuff, too.* The elevator door pinged and Savannah picked up her stride to make it before it left.

The doors opened and Mitch stepped out. He looked at her and smiled.

Savannah skidded to a halt, a scream lodged in her throat.

He ran to her, grabbing her wrist. "Just the person I was looking for."

Terror jolted her to fight and she twisted her arm to escape. "Let me go."

He yanked her to him, giving her a close up view of his sneer. "You don't think I know you talked to your boyfriend."

She glared at him. "He'll be coming after you soon."

Mitch tsked. "I didn't want to hurt you, Savannah. I love you. Why couldn't you just keep your mouth shut?" He dragged her back toward the ballroom. "If you had just done that I never would have known it was you who talked to the FBI."

"I'll scream."

Mitch reached inside his suit jacket and produced a gun. "No, you won't."

He marched her across the ballroom. Savannah's heart pounded, drowning out any ideas on escape. *God, help me.*

As if an answer to her prayer, Carrie appeared from behind the stage. She frowned when she saw Mitch and Savannah. "Hey, I thought you were gone."

Knowing Mitch couldn't see her expression, she widened her eyes and glared at Carrie. "We were just leaving. Are you all done here?"

Carrie gestured behind her. "I'm just grabbing the last of my things."

"Okay."

Carrie stepped to move past them. Mitch shifted so that Savannah remained between Carrie and the gun.

Savannah's brain kicked into gear. "By the way, did you see Mr. Christopher tonight?"

Carrie's steps slowed and put on a puzzled expression, playing the part perfectly. "Now that you mention it, I didn't."

Mitch pressed the gun in her ribs. Savannah kept her tone light. "Me, either. I would be so sad if he missed this. I guess we're going to have to call him and give him an update."

Carrie nodded, her eyes filled with understanding. "Yes, but later. I'm exhausted."

Savannah let out a nervous laugh. "Me, too. Good night."

To Carrie's credit, she managed to take even steps out of the ballroom, but Savannah was sure she would call the police as soon as she got to her phone.

"Let's go." Mitch shoved her forward.

They went around to the entrance behind the stage and took the service stairs down to another long, deserted hallway that led to the back of the hotel. Her dread grew with each step. She couldn't leave here with him. She had no doubt that he would kill her.

When they reached the end of the hallway, Mitch stepped around her and opened the door. The cool evening air instantly chilled her and she wrapped her arms around her shoulders. A large, black car sat at the curb and the door opened when they stepped out.

Savannah slowed.

"Keep moving."

She craned to look at him over her shoulder. "I'm cold, Mitch."

"Put your coat on and keep walking."

Savannah concentrated. She needed to figure out what to do. She unfolded her coat from her arm and shifted her purse from one hand…wait. Her purse. Her phone was in her purse. Maybe once they got into the car, she could figure out how to make a call without Mitch seeing her. She slipped her arms into her coat, doing her best not to bring attention to her purse.

As they walked to the car, a man stepped out of the driver's seat. To Savannah's horror, the trunk popped opened. She sucked in a breath to scream, but Mitch's hand clamped down over her mouth. He snatched her purse from her hand. "You won't be needing that."

Despite her kicking and screaming, Mitch and the other man lifted her with ease and threw her in the trunk. They slammed the trunk before she could scramble out. The car pulled off, the engine drowning out Savannah's screams and sobs. *He's going to kill me.* She took deep breaths, nearly choking off the smell of the exhaust. The fumes seemed to bring a jolt of clarity.

He may kill her, but she was going to do everything she could to stop him. She moved her now free hair out of her face, wriggled around in the darkness so that she was facing the back of the car and went to work on disabling one of the rear tail lights.

*

Jordan yawned for the third time as Will navigated to his mother's brownstone. Will stifled a yawn, drawing his mother's attention.

She laughed. "Why don't you both spend the night at my house tonight. You look exhausted."

Jordan leaned forward so that his head stuck between the front seats. "Can we, Dad?"

Will exhaled. He couldn't deny that it was a tempting offer. "Okay."

"Yay!" Jordan flopped back in the seat.

Will looked at him in the rearview mirror. "Don't think you're off the hook with this running away stuff."

Jordan's head dropped. "I know."

Will parked near his mother's front door and took the key from the ignition. Will took his time climbing out of the car. Jordan, however, bolted out and raced ahead of them and up the stairs.

Denise shook her head. "How does he still have energy?"

Will chuckled and his cell phone rang. "Hello?"

"Agent Anderson." Carrie's voice sounded so forcibly in the phone that Will flinched. "Something has happened to Savannah. She left here with Mitch."

Will stopped up short, his mother staring at him. "Whoa, whoa. Slow down."

"Savannah and Mitch just left here together. She told me in code to call the police." Her speed of her words increased. "I did, but I followed them outside. I saw him put her in the trunk of his car. I already called the police."

Will moaned. *I should have seen her home.* "Don't worry. I'll find her."

"One more thing. Savannah has GPS tracking on her phone. All the employees of Plateau do because of our line of work. I called her phone and it's still on."

"I'm on it."

The world seemed to tilt. He turned to his mother. "Can you watch Jordan tonight?"

Denise frowned. "Of course. What is going on?"

"Savannah is in serious danger. I have to find her."

Denise pressed her hand to her lips. "Oh, no." She gave Will a little push. "Go. I'll tell Jordan you had to go to work."

"Thanks." Will took off in a jog toward the car.

"I'll be praying," his mother called behind him.

I'm going to need it.

Chapter 25

The car slowed. Savannah shifted and held her breath. The fumes from the car caused her head to spin and made her feel like it was still moving. She rolled to her side and the trunk popped open. Despite the fact that it was night, the increased light caused her eyes to water.

They cleared and she saw Mitch standing over her with the gun in his hand. "Get out."

Savannah scooted over the rim of the spare tire that had pressed into her back the whole ride. She slowly climbed out of the car. Her muscles ached.

Mitch snatched her the rest of the way out of the car. "Move it!"

She stumbled forward but regained her balance. "Mitch, you don't have to do this."

His face contorted to a scowl. "You brought this on yourself."

Savannah shrank back, but used the moment to take in her new surroundings. A dilapidated row of warehouses sat to her left. She could hear the sound of cars, but saw none. The parking lot was deserted. She thought she could make out the ramps for what looked like I-295. *That means I'm still in the city.*

Mitch flicked the tip of the gun in the direction of one of the warehouses. "Inside."

Savannah walked as slow as she could, but Mitch stepped up beside her and dragged her faster. "Stop stalling." He almost sounded sad. "Why did you have to talk? We could have been happy together."

He pushed her again and she doubled over, arms pin wheeling. "Do you think I could be happy with you? After all you've done?"

He frowned, like her words had actually wounded him. "We could have been happy, and now I'll have to kill you." He moved to the door, keeping the gun pointed at Savannah, and punched in a code. The door beeped and opened.

Mitch made a sweeping motion. "After you."

Savannah stepped over the low ledge of the door and into the semi-light of the warehouse. The floor was littered with broken pieces of equipment and other industrial trash. She could see the sky through a hole in the ceiling.

"You like my place." Mitch shut the door behind them. "I was planning to use this as the base of my operations here in the DC Metro, but you ruined that."

*I have got to get away from him. Maybe if I—*Savannah's thoughts were cut off by muffled cries and banging.

She turned to find a large metal shipping container sitting in the far corner of the warehouse, near a loading dock. The banging increased and she could make out faint voices. *There are people inside. I have to get them out.*

She whipped back around to face Mitch. "You have to let them go. They are innocent."

Mitch shook his head. "Sorry. They're evidence. Evidence that I have to get rid of...just like you." He stepped around a piece of debris. "Since you're so fond of helping these women, you'll appreciate the irony of dying with them."

He reached for her but she pulled away, planning to run for the door. Before she could, he grabbed a handful of her hair and yanked it. Pain brought tears to her eyes and she screamed.

As she struggled, he dragged her over to the container and turned the locking mechanism on the door. They were greeted with the stench of human excrement when the door swung open. Mitch gave her hair one more strong pull and slung her inside. She tumbled into the container, one of her shoes falling off just before she went in.

She was caught, however, by arms from every direction. The arms righted her. In the dimness of the light, she could just make out the faces of what looked like 30 women looking as frightened as she felt. The door slammed behind her, plunging them into darkness.

Savannah screamed and ran to the door, pounding it with her fist. "Mitch! Mitch, you don't have to do this!"

No answer from the other side.

She leaned against the door and sobbed.

*

Will didn't bother to use care in parking in front of the MPD station. He ran up the stairs, shoes scuffing against the stairs, reminding him that he still wore his tux. He went straight to the desk sergeant. "Is Officer Grant here?" Will turned. "Never mind, I'll find him."

He shot past the desk sergeant despite her protests and found Grant's desk. Grant sprang to his feet when he spotted Will. "What —"

Will pulled out his cell phone. "Savannah Elliott has been kidnapped by the guy behind the brothel. Her assistant called 911 about thirty minutes ago. Has anyone started tracking her number?"

Grant returned to his chair and clicked twice on his mouse. "Give me the number."

Will rattled it off and Grant keyed it into the system. Within seconds, the results popped on the screen. "Looks like it's stationary. Fifteen hundred block of New York Avenue." Grant gave Will a confused look. "Nothing there but empty warehouses."

"Send backup and call Officer Dunn." Will was on the move before he finished speaking.

He ran to the car, fumbling with his keys and dialing Carter at the same time.

Carter answered on the first ring. "Where are you? We've got a lead on Alverez's shipment of women. We think they're at a location on New York Avenue."

Will climbed into the car and slammed the door. "The human right activist that I've been working with, Savannah Elliott, has been kidnapped and taken to that location. She is the daughter of James Elliott, the governor of Georgia." May as well use her father's clout for some good.

"I'll send a team."

Will hung up, threw his phone on the seat beside him, started the car and sped out of the parking lot. *Hang on, Savannah. I'm coming.*

*

Savannah had exhausted all her ideas about how she and the women could escape. She discovered that most of them were Spanish speakers and learned that they trapped inside the container for about 48 hours. Most of them were from Guatemala, like Marisol. They wept as they told her how they had been shipped, but thankfully hadn't been put into brothels yet.

Despite her best attempts to console them, they still cried. Savannah hung to the one piece of consolation she had. *Will was coming.* She was sure of it even though she didn't know how she knew. She was convinced he'd come. The weightier question was would he get to her in time.

Carrie would have gotten the message out to everyone who needed to know…including Will and her parents. She shuddered to think of how they reacted to the revelation of Mitch's true character.

Occasionally, she stepped to the door and listened. Other than a few clanks of metal, she heard nothing else.

She banged on the door again. "Mitch!"

She raised her hand to bang again and paused. A strange light shone through the crack under the door. As she studied it, the smell of smoke reached her nose. Fire.

She renewed her banging. "Mitch!"

Chapter 26

Will whipped his car into the parking lot of the warehouse. He slammed the breaks, grabbed his service weapon from under the seat and hopped out of the car. He studied the warehouses lined up around him. *Which one is she in?*

His wonder only lasted a moment. A plume of smoke drifted above one of the warehouses to his left. He took off in a sprint in that direction.

He rounded a corner and found a black car parked in front of a broken down warehouse. He ran to the door and tried the handle. It clicked open. He stepped back, raised his weapon, pushed the door open with his leg, and stepped inside.

The smell of smoke sent him reeling backwards. The source of the fire, a small flame off to his right, created eerie dancing shadows on the ceiling. He searched for something to put the fire out. "Savannah!"

Almost immediately, he heard banging and screaming. He carefully made his way past the flames and moved in the direction of the noise. "Savannah!" He called again as he drew closer.

Something scraped behind him. He turned to see Mitch approaching. The light from the flames magnified the wild glare in his eyes. Mitch held in his hands what looked like a metal pipe. He raised it, poised to strike. Will moved quick, but not quick enough. Mitch brought the pipe down in vicious swipe. The pipe hit Will's arm with a meaty thud. The pain rattled through Will's bones. His eyes watered. Mitch raised the pipe again and brought it down on Will's shoulder causing him to stumble to the ground.

"Well, look who's here." Mitch circled him. "Came to save your girlfriend?"

And stop you. Will gritted his jaw, raised his weapon and fired one shot. The bullet tore through Mitch's sleeve. The man yelled. The pipe he held fell to the floor with a clang. Mitch dropped to his knees.

Before Mitch could regain his advantage, Will rose. "Where is Savannah?" He leveled his weapon at Mitch.

"Why don't you guess?" Mitch spat with a laugh. "By the time you find her, all of you will be dead from smoke inhalation."

Will glanced at the growing fire. It had crept its way up one side of the wall and licked at the ceiling. *This building is old. It won't take long to burn.* He stepped closer to Mitch. "Tell me where she is!"

Mitch dropped his head and let out a chuckle. Will's heart pounded in his ears.

Mitch looked up. "I don't think so." He sprang forward, tackling Will at the waist. The force drove Will back, his dress shoes skidding on the concrete. Will braced his left foot and brought up his right knee. It connected with a crunch with Mitch's chin.

Mitch's grip loosened. Will raised the butt of his gun and struck Mitch in the back of the head. Mitch groaned and fell face down. Will sprang backwards, refocusing his aim.

Mitch rolled over, grinning at Will. "We can fight all night." He coughed. "Time's ticking."

He began inching backwards. "Savannah!" His words ended with coughing. More banging and yelling.

Mitch slowly rose from the floor. "I have an idea. How about I leave you to your search for Savannah?" He looked over at the door. "I'll just go."

Will did a mental inventory of his pockets. Just his keys and wallet. Not even one zip tie. Will gripped his weapon. Backup should already be outside. They would pick him up as soon as he set foot outside the door. *But what if they're not there.* He couldn't let Mitch walk. More than that, he couldn't let him leave before they found the shipment of girls.

Will narrowed his eyes. "I've got a better idea." He fired another shot, hitting Mitch in the thigh.

Mitch yelled and fell to the ground, writhing in pain.

Will turned in the direction of the banging. Through the smoke, he spotted a container near a loading dock. He ran in that direction. "Savannah!"

This time he could make out voices responding to his call. The fire behind him crackled with intensity. He glanced at the rest of the warehouse. The fire had reached the ceiling and covered most of the front wall. Mitch had managed to slide a few feet from where he'd fallen, a trail of blood following him.

Sweat beaded Will's forehead and he moved to the door of the container. "Savannah!"

"Will! I'm in here!"

Will stooped, grabbed the handles, and swung them upward. The bars at the top of the container let out a squeal. He pulled the doors open and Savannah nearly fell out. She threw her arms around him. "Thank God."

He grasped her hand. "Let's get out of here." He looked over Savannah's shoulder and his heart nearly stopped when he saw women crowding around the opening. Getting Savannah and Mitch out would be challenging enough. How was he going to navigate all these women safely out?

He would have to try. "Come on."

Savannah turned to the frightened faces. "Vamos."

The group moved slowly toward the front door, too slow for Will's liking. A loud crack sounded from above them and a large chuck of flaming ceiling fell in front of them. The women screamed and came to a complete halt.

Savannah gripped his arm. "The loading dock."

Will cast one more glance over his shoulder and tried to spot Mitch through the smoke and flames, but saw nothing. *Maybe he got out.*

He turned the whole group back toward the loading dock. He picked up his pace to a trot, praying the women would follow his example. His heart soared when they did.

The warehouse cooled considerably when they reached the ledge of the loading dock. Will hopped down off the ledge and tried to lift the door. It only budged a little. He turned to Savannah. "Help."

She slid down off the ledge and came to Will's side. Will gave a three count and they heaved the door upwards with all they had. It creaked but only lifted another few inches. Will gritted his teeth, the whimpers of the women fueling him. "Again."

They pulled the door up again. It jolted and shuddered. Then, as if they'd acquired super strength, it shot upwards. Cool air rushed in.

Standing outside the door was Officer Grant with a crowd of MPD officers.

Will let out a shaky laugh. "Dude, I've never been so glad to see you."

Will handed Savannah down to Grant and turned to get the rest of the women out. Will exited last. "Did a man come out the front door? He would have had a gunshot wound in his leg."

Grant shook his head. "Fire was pretty bad out front. That's why we came around here."

Will tilted his head toward Savannah. "Take care of her." He ran back to the loading door and climbed back inside. He heard Savannah screaming his name.

Smoke had almost completely obstructed his view. He reached the container where he'd found Savannah and looked past the burning piece of ceiling that had fallen. Whipping off his jacket, he covered his face and carefully navigated around the flames. His vision blurred with tears and his throat burned. *A few more minutes, Anderson and then get out.* He spied the trail of blood and followed it. He leapt over some debris and moved deeper into the warehouse.

He stopped short.

Mitch lay face up near the door.

Will ran to him and grabbed him under the shoulders. He pulled him toward the door, his mind battling. Mitch had lost a lot of blood. He might be dead. Will didn't have time to check. *Why put your life in danger for him? He deserves to die.* Will pushed the thought away. Mitch's victims deserved to see Mitch punished for his crimes. Will would do everything in his power to make sure that happened.

He let Mitch slump to the ground. Mitch let out a cough. Will opened the door and returned to Mitch. With one last burst of energy, he dragged his body out of the door. As soon as he cleared the door, several of his fellow agents and EMTs rushed to his side. Will stepped back and sighed.

He heard someone yell his name over the din. He turned and saw Savannah running toward him, barefoot. When she reached him, she wrapped her arms around him and he lifted her off the ground.

"Will," she sighed against his neck.

He pressed his face against hers. *Thank you, God.*

Epilogue

Savannah adjusted her veiled tiara for the third time. Even though activity fluttered around her, she remained calm. The wedding planning had been chaotic, but it only reassured her of what she was doing today. She was marrying the man she loved.

Carrie fluffed her veil. "Ready?"

Savannah nodded, her joyful heart threatening to overflow to tears. "Yes."

Her mother and father waited at the end of the hallway. They both smiled when they saw her.

Her mother grasped her hands. "You look lovely."

Tears came to Savannah's eyes at her mother's sincere compliment. Their improved relationship ranked as the best wedding present she could have received, although the improvement was brought on by shock.

Once her parents learned about Mitch's criminal activity, it was their turn to bear the shame. Mitch's involvement in her father's campaign ended up having the impact Savannah suspected it would. In the end, her father had to withdraw his Senate bid because of the public outcry.

Her parent's troubles, however, were not over. They also had to live with several investigations into her father's time as governor and Mitch's trial. Savannah did her best to help them process their emotions, which proved to be great for their relationship.

Daddy kissed her cheek. "I'm so happy for you." He grinned. "Let's get you to that man before his nervousness gets the best of him."

Savannah took her place next to her father. *Will nervous? I doubt it.* As she took her first step down the aisle, she saw what her father meant. Will's expression looked like healthy mix of excitement and anxiety. That didn't remain long once he saw Savannah.

A full smile formed on his face, and on the face of Jordan, who stood as his side as ring bearer. She never expected to have a ready-made family, but she welcomed it. She appreciated being Jordan's stepmom even more after watching Will go through the process of getting legal custody of Jordan. She never imaged that she would find a man with such deep compassion.

Compassion that moved him to fly to Guatemala with Marisol and, with the help of local authorities, shut down that branch of Mitch's operation ring. He'd made sure Marisol's son was returned to her. Marisol, for her gratefulness, had photos taken of Will, herself and her son. Savannah knew without being told that that photo rested inside the pocket of Will's tux.

The walk down the aisle seemed to take forever, but once she arrived at the altar, her father placed her hands in Will's and Savannah smiled at the man who captured her heart.

CPSIA information can be obtained at www.ICGtesting.com
Printed in the USA
BVOW02s1910280116

434648BV00001B/23/P